Silent Praise

An Interracial Christian Romance

Book Three of the "Able to Love" Series

Michelle Lindo-Rice

Michelle Lindo-Rice
P.O. Box 495792
Port Charlotte, FL 33949

This is a work of fiction. Any references or similarities to actual events, real people, living or dead, or to real locales are intended to give the novel a sense of reality. Any similarity in other names, characters, places, and incidents is entirely coincidental.

ISBN-13: 978-1507729557
ISBN-10: 1507729553

Table of Contents

A Note to My Readers

Friends,

Welcome to my world. I am so blessed to bring you *Silent Praise,* the third novel in the "Able to Love" series, where one of the main characters has a disability. Our heroine, Melanie Benson, is deaf because of severe trauma she faced as a child. The strongest theme in *Silent Praise* is that of a Divine plan for our lives. Romans 8: 28 says,

"And we know that all things work together for good to them that love God, to them who are called according to His purpose."

By far, *Silent Praise* is the most emotional read of the three novels in the series. Chase and Melanie are memorable, lovable characters who will need to seek God's face to overcome any hindrances as they find true love.

Before you read this powerful love affair, I'd like to take a moment to share with you an unfathomable love. In John 15:13, Jesus said, "Greater love hath no man than this, that a man lay down his life for his friends." Then he backed up that sentiment with action. Love is an action word. Jesus gave his life so we could have eternal life. What an awesome God! What an amazing sacrifice! I hope you see Him in *Silent Praise.* Please enjoy.

Sincerely,

Michelle Lindo-Rice

Check out sample chapters of my novels and PLEASE join my mailing list at www.michellelindorice.com

Christian Fiction Authors I recommend:

www.blackchristianreads.com

Dedication

For my parents, Pauline and Clive Lindo,
who opened their home and hearts to many.

Prologue

"I can't hold it." Melanie "Lainey" King squeezed her legs together. Crouched over in the dark, she shivered from inside the three-foot oblong closet space. Lainey peered through the folds of the closet door. Her eyes were wide with fear. Mama and Uncle were asleep on the big bed. Lainey slept with Mama unless Uncle came around. Then she had to sleep in the closet.

Lainey's lower body shook. She had to go. *Now.* She pushed the closet door wide and crept outside teenaged mutant ninja turtle style. Lainey inched her way to her mother's bed.

"Mama, I've got to go pee." Lainey whispered as quietly as she could into her mother's ear. She did not want to wake Uncle. His snore bounced off the walls of the room. Lainey twisted her tattered, once-white nightgown, spotted with dingy brown stains. Her lips quivered.

Oh no! A small line of urine trickled down her legs. She cupped her mouth to keep from crying aloud. If she peed on herself, Uncle was going to let her have it. She shook her mother again. "Mama! I've got to go to the bathroom!"

Mama did not budge. But Uncle did.

"What do you want?" He snarled at her into the darkness.

Even through the dark, Lainey could see his hateful eyes.

Uncle jumped and came around the bed to grab her shoulders. "What do you want?"

Lainey's teeth rattled. She opened her mouth but no words came. With a groan, Lainey emptied her bladder. Tears rolled down her face.

"I didn't mean to," she said.

Uncle sniffed. "Did you pee on the carpet?"

Lainey shook her head. "It was an accident."

Uncle bent towards her. His stinky breath hit her in the face. "You're five years old and old enough to stop peeing on yourself! Your mother's bragging how smart you are, says you're reading and writing and all that so you know better. But you know what, you're just plain nasty. Yes, that's right. You're scrawny and nasty, and I can't stand the sight of you."

"Ahhh," Lainey wailed, wiggling her body and holding her head. "Mama," she screamed, but Mama did not hear her.

Uncle dropped Lainey to the ground. He kicked her in the stomach. "I told you what would happen if you peed yourself again because you're too lazy to go to the bathroom."

"I tried to wake Mama," Lainey said. "I can't reach the bathroom light and I'm scared of the dark." Her body shook.

Uncle reached down and snatched her under his arm. "But, no, you want to pee on the floor like you're a dog." He rubbed her face into the urine. "I'll do you like I would a dog."

The pungent smell of her urine hit her nose. Lainey closed her eyes, pinched her lips tight, and closed her mouth. She knew this was the only way to keep from inhaling or swallowing it. Her hair and gown were wet from pee.

Lainey bucked her body to fight her way out of Uncle's strong arms. If he released her, she could run and hide. Her leg kicked him in the groin. With a plop, she landed on the floor.

"You kicked me," Uncle raged.

Like a snake, she slithered under the bed. She saw Mama's legs hit the floor. "Mama!" Lainey yelled.

The lights came on.

"What's going on?" Mama seethed. "What're you doing? Where's Lainey?"

"Your kid peed the floor and I'm tired of it."

Lainey saw his big, white feet at the edge of the bed and cowered into the center.

"Don't you put a hand on her." Lainey heard her mother's yell and relaxed. Mama would save her.

Then, she felt a hand curl around her foot. She stiffened her body and dug her fingers into the ratty carpet. But Uncle's strength outweighed hers. He dragged Lainey from under the bed and picked her up feet first, exposing her.

"Leave her alone," Mama cried, beating at Uncle with her fists.

Uncle dropped Lainey and shoved Mama. Her mother hit the wall and slinked to the floor. Lainey remembered when they moved into this room and Mama had painted the walls bright yellow. Now the yellow was mixed with dirt from tossed food containers and beer cans. Mama's head hung near the big hole from when Uncle punched the wall.

Lainey saw her mother's eyes drift close. Her shoulders sagged. Mama would not be able to help her now. Then Uncle redirected his gaze towards her. Lainey gulped. She scrambled over beer cans. Her tiny hands narrowly missed a sharp needle. Mama said never to touch the cans, needles, or white stuff. Ever.

Uncle kicked the cans out of the way. He grabbed Lainey by the ears and pulled her to stand. His chest heaved. "I'll show you what happens to girls who don't know how to listen." He bunched his fist and hit her right ear.

Lainey screamed and fell to the floor. Her yell made Uncle madder than before; he punched her other ear.

Lainey held her head. "Mama!" Uncle punched and punched her ears. Lainey kicked and scratched at him. "Mama!" Uncle punched again. Blood rolled across her face. "Mama … Mama … *Help me*." Uncle kept punching away at her ears. Tears, snot, and blood made it hard for her to see but Lainey stretched a hand towards her mother. "Mama. Please … help." Lainey went limp. Pain dulled her senses and her eyes closed. For the first time in her life, Lainey was no longer afraid of the dark.

***

Shards of bright light hit her face. Lainey screamed. She woke up kicking and fighting. She remembered Uncle hitting her in the face. She had to stop him. Lainey tried to open her eyes all the way but they hurt. She closed her eyes and clutched her head. There was a bandage around her head.

"Mama!" With effort, Lainey forced her eyes open and looked around the room. Her heart started beating into her chest. *Where am I?* She was hooked up to monitors and she was cold. She shivered. *Where's Mama?* Lainey screamed, afraid to be alone.

A short, brown lady—dark-skinned like her Mama—came over to her. Lainey saw the woman's lips moving but she could not hear anything.

Lainey panicked. "I can't hear you. My ears are closed. I can't hear you." She grabbed her ears. "Ahhh! I'm trying to scream but I can't hear myself."

The lady nodded and said something. Since she could not hear, Lainey focused on the woman's kind face. The lady wrapped Lainey in her arms.

Lainey stilled. *This lady won't hurt me.* Lainey welcomed her soft touch. The lady lowered Lainey back to the bed and bunched the covers around her. Lainey felt a soft kiss on the top of her head.

Then the doctor came in. Lainey knew him. He had fixed her broken arm and stitched her busted lip. She was so glad to see someone she recognized. "I know you! You're Dr. James," Lainey said. She knew she said the words right because she saw him nod his head.

"I can't hear myself, Dr. James," Lainey said. "Can you fix my ears?"

The lady covered her mouth with her hand.

"Why is she crying?" Lainey's eyes filled with tears. She looked at Dr. James. "I want my mama."

For some reason, her words made the lady cry even more. A tall, skinny brown man entered the room and the lady ran into his arms, burying her face in his chest.

Lainey looked at Dr. James. "Please stitch my ears so I can hear. And, can you tell Mama where I am? She might be looking for me." She was surprised to see Dr. James wipe his eyes.

She saw the needle he held and tried to move. "Mama said no needles!" She wiggled to the edge of the bed away from Dr. James. But Dr. James held her down. The last thing Lainey felt was the pierce from the needle, and then her eyes closed.

1

"Dratted snooze button," Melanie muttered, adjusting her Ray Ban's. It was close to 7:30 a.m. but the sun made its presence known. "I just had to press snooze one more time."

Boy did she regret her Thursday night *Twilight* binge. Melanie had stayed up until 2:00 a.m. re-watching the four movies in the *Twilight* saga. Edward, Jacob, and Bella had filled her thoughts. What she would give to be in Bella's shoes. She wanted two hot men fighting over her. Heck, she would even settle for one not-so-hot guy calling her ever so often. In the small town of Port Charlotte, pickings were slim, especially for someone with a disability.

Melanie blew her curls out of her face and zipped her grey Infiniti across the lanes. It was mid-January, peak season for snowbirds. The normally scanty traffic lanes on US 41 were packed with Canadian license plates. *Where were all these people going at this hour? Aren't they supposed to be retired?*

Melanie saw the amber light ahead and hit the accelerator. She could not miss the light or she would be late and Nancy would be in her face. Melanie whizzed through the light right before it switched to red. She made a fist. *Yes!* She put on her indicator to make the left turn on Cochran Blvd. Melanie escalated to catch the green turning arrow. She glanced at the clock. She had two minutes to spare. Then she looked into the rearview mirror.

Her eyes widened. Red and blue lights twinkled behind her. Moving at a snail's pace, Melanie pulled into the mini mall. Because of the early hour, there weren't many cars in the lot. Besides the Wells Fargo, there was a Books-A-Million, Staples, Big Lots, and a McDonald's. She hoped the officer would keep going. But he followed her. She rolled her eyes and pulled into a parking space.

Great. Not only was she late, she was also going to be ticketed right outside her job. Melanie served as a bank loan officer and investment banker. Her manager stayed on her butt. *Lord, please, now would be a good time for you to show up and show out.*

Melanie looked into her left side mirror. She saw tall, muscular legs unfold out of the unmarked police car. He had to be at least 6'3" with light brown hair cropped low on his head. He whipped off his sunglasses. Melanie took hers off as well.

She stole another glance. *Mr. Officer is fine.* She watched his confident stride. This man should be strutting on a runway somewhere. It was a sin he had his body covered under that green uniform, although he wore it well. She peeked at her reflection in the mirror. Her curls were in disarray. Melanie ran her fingers through the strands before giving up.

The officer tapped on the glass. Melanie jumped even though she knew he was coming. She plastered a smile on her face and lowered her window. She could smell the McDonald's biscuits and coffee. Her stomach rumbled. There was no way she would have time to hit the drive-thru.

Melanie made sure to keep her eyes on his lips. The officer's mouth parted to reveal white teeth and a beautiful smile.

"License and insurance," he said.

Her breath caught. His sharp green eyes made her think of running through the lush fields on a hot Florida day. She tore her eyes away and dug into her brown, oversized Coach bag for her wallet. Her hands shook. This was only her second time being pulled over.

Melanie handed the officer her information.

She observed him keenly, noting the exact moment he saw she was deaf. He shot her a quick, sympathetic glance. Melanie stiffened her shoulders and tossed her hair. "Are you going to give me a ticket?" she asked.

Her voice must have bellowed because he stepped back. "You can speak?"

Melanie covered her eyes with her hands. The sun was already out and viciously making its presence felt.

"I also read lips." This time she spoke above a whisper, she hoped. She squinted her eyes to read his name badge—Officer Chase Lawson. His name suited him.

"Where are you rushing to this morning, Ms. Benson?" he asked, making sure she could see his mouth.

Hearing the surname *Benson* jolted Melanie's

memory. She had a flashback of laying in the hospital bed. When Mama awakened from her stupor the next morning, she had taken Lainey to the emergency room. Melanie remembered her mother's screams and terrified eyes. That was the last memory she had of her mother. Melanie found our Janet had been arrested and she never saw her again.

And as for Uncle, he disappeared.

The lady and gentleman in her room that day were Gary and Rhoda Benson, her foster parents. They adopted her and gave her their name and a new life.

Melanie scrunched her nose. *Why am I remembering this now?*

The officer lightly touched Melanie's shoulder to get her attention.

Melanie started. The officer had a hand on his hip, waiting for her answer. She pointed to the bank.

He smiled revealing a set of beautiful teeth. Officer Lawson patted her hand that was resting on the steering wheel. Electricity shot through her spine. Her eyes widened. *Had he felt that?* Melanie affixed her gaze on his hand.

His thumb caressed hers. He must have caught himself because he removed his hand. "I'm letting you go with a warning," Officer Lawson said. He made sure she saw his lips.

Did he spare me because I'm deaf? Melanie bristled, "Just give me the ticket if I deserve it."

He shook his head. "Are you going to argue with me because I'm giving you a break?"

She thought of the points on her license and her insurance bill. He was right. Why was she even arguing? "No, Officer," Melanie said. "I'll be sure to go to bed on time tonight."

He gave a little smile and held out his hand to return her documents to her. "See that you do that."

Their hands met. This time there was no denying the electric bolt shooting through her system. Her eyes met his. She knew he felt it too. His eyes narrowed. Officer Lawson looked around the still empty parking lot. Then he bent lower so she could see his mouth.

"Melanie?"

She lifted a brow and nodded.

"Listen, I know this is unconventional and in my seven years on the job, I've never done this." His eyes met her brown ones. He laid that smile on her again. "I'm Chase Lawson." He held out his hand. Melanie touched his hand briefly.

Her heart thumped but she made a point to look at her watch before looking back at him. *Spit it out.*

"Would you like to meet up for a cup of coffee sometime?" he asked. "I'm feeling a connection here and I'd like to explore it further—"

Melanie shook her head. "I can't."

Chase held a hand up. "Oh, sorry. I should have asked if you're seeing someone." She watched a red hue build on his face.

"I'm not," Melanie said. She jutted her chin. "I don't like cops. Thanks for the warning, *Officer*. Now, if you'll excuse me, I'm late for work."

Melanie opened her door and slammed it with a decisive shut. Her caramel-toned skin reddened when she saw her floral skirt was caught in the door. Melanie opened the door to retrieve her skirt.

Chase tapped her on the back.

"Have a nice day," he said. She saw Chase's pearly whites and knew he was laughing at her.

Melanie ignored him and held her head high as she walked away. But she had an extra sway in her hips as she made her way toward the bank. Her best friend, Rachel Morrison, let her inside. Melanie turned around to see if Chase was looking, however, he was already in his car. She swallowed her disappointment.

"I see you were pulled over, Miss Speedy," Rachel said.

Melanie and Rachel were high school friends. The two of them, plus Tricia Yang, her adopted sister, made up the Tres Amigas.

"I almost got a ticket," Melanie breathed out, smoothing out her fuchsia blouse.

Dressed in a tailored navy blue business suit with matching sandals, Rachel flipped her shoulder-length blond hair. "He could write me up any time," she said, doing a two-step.

Melanie giggled. "You're such a flirt."

"Yes, and I'm proud of it." Her hazel eyes sparkled. "If that were me, I'd have his number."

Melanie pictured Chase's smile and those green eyes. "Actually, he asked me out, but I turned down," she said.

Rachel furrowed her brows. "That was one fine man. You could've given him a chance."

"I don't do cops." She glared. "You know why." Although, she agreed Chase was one hot cop.

Rachel nodded. "I do, but I don't agree."

"You don't have to. I'm the one who has to live with my decision. Not you. Between work and my other commitments, I don't have time for dating." Melanie made her way to her office and turned on the light. Rachel must have followed her because Melanie felt a tap on her back.

She groaned and faced her friend.

"You don't mind Emory," Rachel said. "He's a police officer."

"He's different, and he's Tricia's husband. Plus we knew Emory when he was pimpled with thick glasses and braces."

"True, but he's now a perfect 10. Who knew Emory would've morphed into such a hunk?"

Rachel's smiled faded. She focused on something behind Melanie. Or rather, someone. Melanie swung around. She resisted the urge to roll her eyes. Their boss, Nancy Devries, headed their way. Rachel waved at Nancy before going into the adjacent office.

"Melanie, I need to speak with you," Nancy said.

Melanie took in Nancy's frumpy grey dress. *Which dumpster did Nancy find that in?* "I have a busy day ahead of me."

"This can't wait. You approved a couple of loans

without my approval."

Lord, I don't have time for Nancy's nitpicking. Melanie looked at her watch. The bank was about to open. "How about we meet at 12:30? I have a couple of investment consultations and two loan reviews this morning."

Nancy bit her lip. "I'll see you then." Her eyes swept Melanie's outfit. "You look colorful."

"And you look ..." Melanie scanned Nancy's frizzy red hair and ugly brown flats. She could not think of something nice to say. So she said nothing.

Nancy's mouth popped open before she stomped off.

Melanie felt a hand tap her shoulder.

"Couldn't you be nice? You're a child of God. You know better," Rachel said.

"Yes, I'm a child of God but I'm not a doormat. Nancy only double-checks my work. She signs off on your stuff without a second glance. But she scrutinizes everything I do." Melanie used sign language for her next comment. "She's racist and you know it."

Rachel shook her head. "She's jealous. Nancy almost got fired when she messed up that money transfer. You would've been her replacement," Rachel signed back.

A customer entered the bank and Rachel went to greet him. Melanie was glad for the interruption. She wandered back into her office to get started on her day. But, ever so often, Chase's smiling face flashed before her. She touched her hand where his hand had rested.

Then she pushed him out of her mind. Her life was too busy for romance—and romancing a cop was out of the question.

2

"Tell me you didn't tell him that," Tricia Yang signed. She flipped her butt length braids. Her half-inch length nails got tangled in her hair.

"She did. A gorgeous cop asked her out and she turns him down flat," Rachel said.

The three women were at Tricia and Emory's three bedroom home that Saturday night. They attended church together at Ransomed Hope Seventh Day Baptist on Saturday mornings and usually ended up at each other houses afterwards. Tricia's husband, Emory, worked as a Sheriff for Lee County. Since Emory was working a night shift, Melanie and Rachel would stay over for a pamper session.

All three women knew sign language. They used a combination of sign language and voice to communicate. Of the three, Tricia signed the most, even though she had a cochlear implant. She liked to keep her skills fresh as she worked as a paraprofessional in a classroom for deaf and hard-of-hearing students at Peace River Elementary.

The women sat cross-legged on the brown industry-type carpet in the living room. They had cotton between their freshly painted toes. The 60-inch TV had a reality show of wanna-be-models on, but the women were not paying attention.

"You know Melanie would *never* date a cop," Tricia said. "It was months before she accepted Emory in my life. At least three people on his job has asked her out and she has turned them down."

However, Chase was the first one Melanie had regrets about. "Emory was all right until he decided to become a cop," she said.

Tricia laughed.

Rachel held up a hand. "The cops who hauled your mother off to jail were doing their j-o-b. It wasn't their fault. It was Janet's. She neglected you. You should've given Officer Chase a chance. That's all I'm saying."

Melanie rolled her eyes. "Why are you worried about my love life, or lack of one?" There was more to her dislike for cops than that, but Melanie kept that information to herself.

"Because we hate to see you alone. Ever since Dad had his heart attack, you've retreated into yourself. It's like you're afraid of living," Tricia answered.

Melanie shook her head. "That's not true."

"You reneged on your lease to move back home," Tricia said.

"Mom needed my help," Melanie defended.

Rachel chimed in. She made sure Melanie could see her lips. "You gave up your chance for Juilliard. Melanie, you should be in Manhattan dancing on Broadway. You shouldn't be withering away here in this small backwards town called Port Charlotte."

"I'm not withering away. You guys are making it sound as if I'm this old spinster with a million cats around me. I'm an investment banker. I have my MBA. I'm doing very well."

Rachel pulled away and laughed. "You'll be that spinster scratching her bottom with rollers in her hair if you don't find someone."

"Look at you," Melanie said. "You aren't dating anyone."

Rachel's face reddened. "I've dated. I am dating, sort of."

Melanie straightened. "You're seeing someone?"

"Why haven't we heard about this person?" Tricia asked.

The doorbell rang distracting them from their conversation.

"There's our pizza," Tricia said. She hobbled to the kitchen where her purse hung on the back of the wooden chair.

"You sure you don't need some money?" Melanie asked.

Tricia signed, "No worries. I've got it. You bought the last time and the time before that."

Melanie nodded. "I don't mind."

"Let me get the paper plates and cups," Rachel said. She rushed into the kitchen.

Melanie was not fooled. Rachel was trying to avoid the question.

Tricia paid for their three pies and soda, and placed them on the glass coffee table she had purchased at a yard sale.

Melanie blew on her toes before reaching for hand sanitizer in her bag. She longed for a slice of pizza. She was a cheese lover and would eat pizza every day if she could.

She cleaned her hands and snagged a slice.

Rachel returned with the paper goods and napkins. Melanie noticed Tricia was on the phone. Talking to Emory, no doubt.

Melanie finished off her slice and reached for another. She gave Rachel a pointed stare. "So who is this boyfriend?"

Rachel turned her head away. Melanie knew it was on purpose. She tapped Rachel's foot. "Tell me."

"He's no one. It's complicated," Rachel signed. For some reason, she could not look Melanie in the eyes. Rachel ate her pizza taking mouse-size bites.

Seeing her discomfort, Melanie dropped the issue. Rachel would tell her when she was ready.

"Pastor's message was on point today," Tricia said, after she ended the call.

Melanie welcomed the conversation change. "Yes, my fingers hurt from all the notes I took."

Pastor Brooks used a sign-language interpreter since his sermons were televised. Melanie was grateful for this accommodation. Her parents had ruled out many other assemblies because they did not have an interpreter.

"I felt like when he talked about Ruth and Naomi, he was talking about me," Tricia said. "I wonder what my life would have been like if the Benson's hadn't adopted me."

"I'd be dead," Melanie said.

"I'm so grateful God brought them into my life." Tricia's eyes brimmed with tears. "I don't know why I'm so emotional."

Melanie understood. When Tricia was twelve, she had the option of returning to her birth mother. Her mother had kicked the drugs and worked in a fast-food chain. The Bensons had sat both girls down to give them the news.

Tricia said, "Don't make me leave. I like my life here with you guys. You're my parents. You introduced me to God and a better life. I am home."

Rhoda hugged Tricia with tears in her eyes. "As long as you want, you have a home here."

"You can still have a relationship with your mother," Gary offered.

Tricia nodded. "I would like to get to know her. I know when Peggy abandoned me it was the drugs. It wasn't her."

Melanie remembered being awed at Tricia's big heart. Tricia and Peggy were still in touch. Tricia knew her other brothers and sisters and spent time with them.

Rhoda had urged Melanie to reach out to her mother but Melanie refused. Janet King was in prison and Melanie believed she should stay there.

Suddenly Tricia clutched her stomach. She bolted to

her feet and raced to the bathroom. Both Melanie and Rachel abandoned their slices. They scurried to stand outside the bathroom door.

"What's happening?" Melanie signed.

"She's throwing up," Rachel signed back. She gagged and covered her mouth.

Melanie scrunched her nose. There were times she was glad she could not hear. "You think it's a virus?" This time of year, many children became sick. Their runny noses and dirty hands made them virus-spreading machines. Tricia could have caught a bug from one of the students.

"I think it might be a nine-month virus," Rachel said.

Melanie's eyes widened. "Oh."

They waited by the door until Tricia came out. Her face was flushed and her eyes teary. Melanie smelled peppermint. She was glad Tricia had brushed her teeth.

"I guess this is a good time for me to tell you I'm expecting," Tricia said. "I'm about two months along."

Rachel waved her hands excitedly. She did this instead of screaming for Melanie's benefit. The women hugged and jumped up and down. Then they huddled together, rubbing Tricia's stomach.

Seeing Tricia's joy, Melanie felt a twinge. Tricia had worked through her past and now she was in a wonderful relationship.

Chase's face came before her. Melanie wondered if he was her chance; her chance at happiness. That thought stayed with her all night.

When she returned home that Sunday, Melanie pulled into the Benson's residence. Her parents lived in what was known as a mother-daughter home. Melanie exited her car and entered through her separate entrance to a living area. She stepped into her living room. She had thrown matted rugs on the wooden floors. She had found her lima bean colored leather sofa and chair at a garage sale. Her coffee table and end table were hand-me-downs from when her mother re-decorated. But the 55-inch TV was all hers.

Her apartment also featured a master bedroom, bathroom, and a kitchenette she rarely used. Melanie saw no reason to cook. Rhoda always had something scrumptious warming in the oven on her side of the house.

At the moment, Melanie's eyes were glued on a letter at her feet. Her mother must have slipped it under her door. Melanie bent to pick up the letter, knowing it was from Janet.

With a sigh, she sauntered into her bedroom. She sat on the queen-sized bed, opened her nightstand drawer, and added the letter to the others. Unopened. Un-read.

3

"You didn't have to come today. Gary's doing much better. I don't want you taking off work, especially on a Monday," Rhoda said.

Melanie piled scrambled eggs on her plate. "Mom, I'm coming. You say this every time. I have tons of vacation time. I could take three months off and get paid. Taking a day to check on my father's heart is nothing for me to do. And, it doesn't matter if it's a Monday."

"I'm worried. When I worked as a cashier for Beall's, I was never late. I never took days off." Rhoda puffed her chest. "I even went to work sick."

Melanie reached for her toast. "Well, those days are long gone, Mom."

Rhoda shrugged. "I don't know why I argue with you anyway. Once you've made up your mind ..."

"Exactly. So let's drop it," Melanie said. "I want to be here."

"I feel guilty. I feel like you've given up so much because of us." Rhoda's lip quivered.

Melanie hugged her mom briefly. "I didn't give up anything. You and Dad opened your heart and home to me. You raised me right. I have a lucrative career.

Because of some wise investment decisions I have more money in the bank than I can spend in this lifetime. I'm blessed and I thank God for you."

Rhoda's eyes misted. "You're a blessing to us, too. When you came to us, you were this tiny, scrawny kid. Now look at you, towering over me. You're beautiful."

Gary strolled into the kitchen. His brown shirt was tucked into his tan slacks. "What are you two boohooing about?" he signed.

"Mom's being emotional again," Melanie joked.

"I'm just grateful, honey," Rhoda signed. "Our daughter paid off our house note and she's paying your hospital bills. I'm overwhelmed. We're the parents and we should be taking care of her. Not the other way around." She pointed to the table and said, "Have your oatmeal. I already ate."

"I'm grown. I can take care of myself," Melanie countered.

"You heard her, Rhonda. She's grown." Gary kissed Melanie's forehead. She beamed. There's no denying she was daddy's girl.

Gary slid into a chair to have his oatmeal. Melanie joined him. Rhoda placed turkey bacon strips on Melanie's already full plate. Gary eyed Melanie's meal.

"Want to trade?" he signed.

Melanie laughed. "You know you can't eat this."

"Oh, yeah. Watch me." Gary swiped a slice of bacon. He bit half before Melanie could stop him.

Rhoda swatted Gary's arm. "Behave yourself. We're

going to the heart doctor today. I need you on your best behavior."

Gary nodded but when Rhoda turned her back to get their tea, he winked at Melanie.

Melanie smiled. This was the best part of being home. Watching her parents together and so in love. She thought of Janet's letter and frowned. Her life would have been *so* different had she stayed with Janet. God knew what He was doing when He made adoption.

Rhoda must have read her mind because she asked, "Did you see Janet's letter?"

Melanie rolled her eyes. "Yes, I did."

"Let me guess. It's stuffed into your nightstand with the others."

"I don't know why I keep them. I should throw them in the bin." Melanie stuffed the eggs into her mouth. Yum. Her mouth was in heaven. They were fluffy with the right amount of seasoning.

Rhoda grabbed a paper towel and wiped her hand. "Don't throw them away. I'm praying you'll change your mind and read them one day."

"She will. When she's ready, Rhoda," Gary said. He swiped another piece of bacon from Melanie's plate.

Melanie made a point to look at her watch. "We have to leave in ten minutes. Can we talk about something else? I don't want indigestion while I eat."

"I have something else to talk about. Your dancing. You should get back into it," Rhoda said. "As you said, you have enough money for a lifetime so you can afford to pursue your dream."

Melanie bit into her toast and chewed. She was used to this debate and could repeat her parents' words verbatim.

"I have to agree with your mother," Gary said. "You need to be dancing. It's because of me why you're not performing on stage. Look at Misty Copeland. She's making a name for herself and putting black people in history books."

Melanie thought of Misty, the first black ballerina. "I'm not a ballerina. I'm a contemporary dancer and I do dance. I'm at the studio so much, I could move in. Delia and Hank blessed me with my own keys so I can come and go as I please. I'm fine. I promise you that." Opposite to her words, Melanie's heart wrenched. She was young enough to get back into dance, or open a dancing school. Then she pushed the feelings aside and finished her breakfast. She gathered her and Gary's breakfast plates and put them in the sink.

"I'm glad the Hartman's gave you your own keys, but you need your own—"

Melanie gave Rhoda a hard stare. "Leave it alone, Mom. Please."

Rhoda rolled up her sleeves. Melanie placed a hand on her mother's shoulder. "I'll do the dishes later. I promise. We have to be at Advance Imaging by nine." She hustled her parent's out the door.

Gary's visit with the cardiologist went well. His EKG was uneventful. There had been no 'episodes' noted. Episodes or events referred to mild heart attacks a person could have without knowing it. Melanie slumped with relief. Dr. Zhivago released Gary from mandatory three-month checkups to six-month checkups.

"Hallelujah!" Rhoda rejoiced. She didn't care who saw her. "God is a healer."

"God's not ready for me, yet," he said. Her parents kissed and Gary wiped at a tear in his eye.

Once they were back inside the vehicle, before Melanie started the car, Rhoda signed, "See, honey. God is clearing the path for you to get back to your life."

Melanie rolled her eyes. "I like my life and I like making money. I have to make money, Mom."

Gary's medical bills were astronomical. She was not hurting in the finances department, but Melanie had to replenish. Growing up in extreme poverty and hungry for the first years of her life, Melanie needed the comfort money provided. That's why she had gone into investment banking. She liked knowing she could afford anything she wanted. She liked being able to help her parents and others.

Though Melanie liked making money, she *loved* dancing. One was her play toy and one was her passion. Nevertheless, she was not ready to choose. Not yet.

Rhoda held Melanie's face in her hands. "You have everything you could ever want," Rhoda said. "I know deep inside you're still scared you'll wake up to the nightmare of your life before us. I know you were hungry and starved, but God has delivered you. You'll never hunger or thirst again."

"I thought I was safe and I almost lost Dad,"

Melanie said. "If you hadn't found him when you did
…"

Rhoda had entered their bathroom to put away
towels when she saw Gary slumped over on the toilet.

Gary tapped Melanie on the shoulder. "I'm here,
and I'm not going anywhere."

"I … I can't take that chance," Melanie whispered.

"Don't do God's job for Him," Rhoda said. "He's
got us in His hands."

Melanie knew her mother was right, but her faith
was weak. One day she was with her biological mother
and the next Janet was gone. Taken away from her,
forever. Back then she had been a helpless child. Now
she would do everything in her power to keep that
from happening again.

4

"She doesn't do cops? What does that mean?" Judd "The Hulk" Armstrong asked Chase.

Judd took a sip of his coffee. He drank his coffee, "Black like I am," Judd would say. From Chase's first day on the job, Judd had shown him the ropes. Originally from Baton Rouge, Louisiana, Judd had introduced Chase to Jambalaya, gumbo, oxtail soup, and other spicy cuisine. He was the only African-American on staff at the District 2 office in Port Charlotte, but Judd was not intimidated. He made sure he did his job and he did it well.

"I have no idea what that means. I was on my way back from the jailhouse when I saw her speeding," Chase said. It had been a long night extraditing two inmates from the precinct to the jailhouse in Punta Gorda. It was not the distance, it was the paperwork. "After pulling double duty, I had to get home and sleep. Besides, my mother taught me right. A girl only has to tell me no once."

Judd waggled his eyebrows. "Sometimes no means yes. But, you're too holy now to know what that means."

Chase shrugged. "I'm trying to live right by God."

"Can't argue with that," Judd said.

Judd's desk was adjacent to Chase's. It was piled

high with folders, papers, pictures, and a bonsai plant. Somewhere under the pile of papers lie a small pit-bull made out of pine. Chase had carved it for Judd who wanted a dog, but did not have the time to care for one.

Judd had been touched by Chase's gesture. Chase shrugged it off. Whittling wood was a hobby. Nevertheless, Judd treasured his dog and named it The Snapster. But by far, Judd's most prized possession was his son's picture. Devin lived in Louisiana with his mother.

In contrast, Chase's desk was clutter free. He had a few carved pieces of dolphins and birds but no pictures. He kept his personal life, personal.

Chase sipped his Earl Grey tea and mused. "First time I ask someone out like that and she shot me down. Maybe she's leery to date a cop—what with all the Eric Garner protests and the Trayvon Martin shooting—cops have a bad rap. Plus I'm white."

Judd threw back his head and laughed. "Look at you being sorry you're white. Like being white will ever be a negative."

Chase knew his face was beet red. "I'm not sorry I'm white—"

Judd rolled his chair to Chase's desk. He thumped Chase on the back. "I'm only messing with you. For a woman to say that, it must be personal."

"Whatever the reason, she turned down my invite." Chase closed his eyes. He could see Melanie's smooth, brown skin; her tight, shoulder-length curls; and her slight gap when she smiled. He opened his eyes to find Judd staring at him. "What?"

"What's her full name?" Judd clicked his screen. "I'm going to pull her up to get a good look at her."

Before Chase could answer, Lieutenant Marc Robards, the District 2 Commander, strode over to them. He had a file in his hand. Judging by the thinness, Chase knew this was a new case.

Fit and lean, Lt. Robards updated them. "We have an Amber alert. A missing boy, Steven Ashton. Five years old. Last seen wearing khaki shorts and a blue and green striped shirt. Near Chamberlain and Biscayne. The Ashton's live in a dense area. They think Steven might have wondered off into the woods. Steven's also deaf. There are three sexual predators within ten miles of his home. *Three.* I have a frantic mother I need a statement from. A couple of rookies took the call but you two need to get out there. The father is out searching in the woods." Marc pinned his grey gaze on Chase and handed him the file. "I want this child found. Yesterday."

Goose bumps rose on Chase's arm. A missing child and pedophiles were not a good combination. He gripped the manila folder. "We're on it."

Chase and Judd jumped to their feet. Judd tossed his unfinished cup of coffee into the trashcan.

"He's deaf," Judd remarked, off-handedly. "What are the odds you'd meet two deaf people in the same day." He made his way out the front door.

Nothing just happened.

Chase knew that from experience. He pondered Judd's words as he followed him out the precinct. The Florida sun pelted his skin and Chase whipped out his sunglasses. It was almost noon. Ashton could face dehydration, snakebite, or worse—alligators.

Lord, please watch over Steven and please give me the tools to find him, Chase prayed internally. His meeting Melanie was no accident. She knew sign language. God knew this would happen and he provided her.

Chase's heart beat with anticipation. He had a good reason to see Melanie again. If only the reason was not because of such dire circumstances.

While Judd drove, Chase reviewed the file. Dr. Francis Ashton and his wife, Nadine, lived with their only son, Steven. Nadine said Steven was playing in their yard when she ran inside to use the restroom. One minute later she returned to find the yard empty and her son gone.

Twenty minutes later, Chase and Judd drove down a long driveway and pulled up to the house worthy of a *Better Homes & Garden* magazine. There were six other cop cars parked outside the home. The men exited the patrol car and walked toward the house.

Judd whistled. "Look at this place. There has to be at least two acres of land here."

Chase gave a perfunctory knock and another officer opened the door. Judd crooked his head signaling he was going to walk the perimeter of the house.

"Detective Lawson?" the officer said.

Chase nodded.

"Come with me."

Chase made sure to wipe his shoes on the doormat before entering the home. He slowed his steps as he approached a diminutive woman perched on the edge of a white couch. In fact, everything in the room was white, from the plush white throw rugs on the wooden floor to the coffee table. If it weren't white, then it was sterling silver. He saw several frames with pictures of Steven, but he did not touch them. Chase noted the absence of toys and other paraphernalia that said a child lived there. In fact the room was spotless.

Nadine Ashton's orange dress was the only splash of color in the room. She held tissues in her hand. Her body shook from crying. She raised puffy eyes to greet him. Despite her being upset, Chase noted Nadine Ashton's beauty. Her jet-black hair and large, brown eyes could give Kim Kardashian serious competition.

"I didn't do it," she said. "I didn't harm my son. He … wandered off and … Steven could be lost … or … I…" Then she pointed an accusatory finger toward a female officer, "Yet, *she* is busy questioning me instead of looking for my child."

"Mrs. Ashton?" Chase asked.

"Please call me Nadine," she said. Nadine hiccupped and blew her nose.

"Nadine, I know these questions seem mundane, but it helps. Every question is important. I'm sure you want to find your son."

She nodded. "I do. I wanted to be out there searching with my husband." She jumped to her feet. "I have to use the restroom."

"Go ahead. I'll be right here."

Chase signaled to the other officers to leave. He retrieved his notepad and pen, took a seat, and ran his hand along the edge of the couch. He had no doubt that it was imported from Italy.

"Detective, care if we move this to the kitchen?" Nadine asked.

Chase stood. He gestured to her to lead the way. Her heels clicked on the floor as they made their way into the back of the house.

He stepped from the hallway and breathed in. Something smelled good. A Hispanic housekeeper gave him a brief, sad smile. Chase liked this cheery room. The warmth and the deep apple and gold colored trimmings said home to him. He saw toys stacked in a corner. "I baked apple pies. I'm so nervous; I didn't know what to do. Mrs. Ashton said I must keep busy, so … I'll cut you both a slice."

"Thanks, Selena." Nadine ambled over to the table. She pushed aside coloring books and scattered crayons. "Steven loves color. He could spend days …" Another fresh bout of tears followed. Nadine looked through the huge glass windows at the playground before turning her glassy eyes toward him. "Steven was outside on the monkey bars. Selena was cleaning, and I was in here. I rushed right there," she said, pointing to a small door, "and I used the bathroom. I wasn't in there but a minute …"

"What time was it?"

"A little after ten. Steven had spent the night coughing so I decided to keep him home. He attends Myakka River Elementary," Nadine said. She spoke under her breath. "I wish I had listened when Francis suggested we fence the area. But, look at where we are." She swept her hands. "Nothing out here for days. I thought it was safe …"

"Even if there was a fence, if someone wanted to enter the yard, they could jump the gate."

Nadine nodded but Chase knew she was not consoled. From his vantage point, he saw Judd approaching from the woods. Chase cleared his throat and changed the subject.

"Tell me about your husband. What does he do?"

"Francis is an oral surgeon. He splits his time between North Port and Sarasota. I have an MBA in business but once I had Steven I decided to stay at home." Her breath caught. "Steven was born deaf but he is full of life. There's nothing he won't do or try. My husband and I refused to let Steven's disability limit him. But he can't hear. He can't hear us trying to find him." She wiped her face.

Selena brought over two huge chunks of apple pies and placed them on the table. Chase reached for the smaller of the two pieces. Nadine gave the pie a cursory glance but did not touch hers. Judd rapped on the glass door. Selena went to let him inside. Chase gave Judd a hopeful look.

"Did they find him?" Nadine asked. She was halfway out of her seat.

"No. A news team is setting up outside. Your husband is going to make a plea. We have a picture of Steven. Do you want to join him?" Judd sat in one of the vacant chairs at the table. Selena brought him a generous slice before saying she was going to clean the china. Judd dug into his slice.

Nadine shook her head. "I don't think I can do it

without falling apart."

"Are you and your husband happy?" Chase knew his question caught her off guard.

Nadine shifted. She did not meet his gaze. "We have our ups and downs like any other couple. But no major issues. What does it matter anyway? This is about our son, not us."

"Sometimes one or more parents are involved when a child goes missing," Judd said.

Chase prodded further. "You said you had no major issues. Did you have any recent arguments or concerns?"

She made a show of pushing her pie across her plate. "We argued about money."

Chase and Judd snapped to attention.

"Francis made some bad investments. He wanted to touch Steven's trust fund—my parents and I set those up for him. I told Francis no. I have my own money and he's not getting his hands on it. Francis stormed off. But I know him. Francis would never harm Steven. He wouldn't do this, I tell you."

Chase wrote down her words.

"Where did your husband go when he left you this morning?" Judd asked. He finished off his slice.

She shrugged. "I don't know. His office, probably," she mumbled. "That's where he spends most of his time."

Chase caught the barb in Nadine's tone. The Ashton's were having major issues. "Do you know anything about his investments?"

Nadine shook her head. "I don't know and right now, I don't care about Francis' money troubles. I can barely think about that. I want my son!" She banged her fists on the table and broke down. "Steven's been gone for three hours. Three hours. He must be hungry or … hurt … I don't know where he is." Her shoulders shook from her vehement wails.

Judd reached over to comfort the hysterical woman. Chase went to pour her a glass of water.

"Nadine, I know this is difficult but your answers are really helping," Chase said, handing her the glass.

She sobbed. "Helping? It sounds like you think my husband did it." Nadine gulped on the water.

"We can't be sure of that," Jude said.

Chase gritted his teeth. He was sure. Francis Ashton was behind his son's disappearance. He would bet his career on it.

"My parents are flying in from Martha's Vineyard. They plan to offer a hundred thousand dollars reward. It was Francis' idea," Nadine whispered.

Judd's eyes were as wide as his. "Let's wait before broadcasting that." Judd released Nadine. "I'm going to sweep Steven's room and take another look around the house. Where is it?"

Nadine gave him directions.

"Who was his investment banker?" Chase asked.

Nadine wiped her face. "His papers are in his study. I'll get them." She rushed off to get the documents.

Chase observed the media frenzy near the playground. He wandered outside. Dr. Francis Ashton approached the makeshift podium. Chase studied him. He needed to have a talk with the doctor. Chase had a hunch. Francis held all the answers.

He bent his head. If he were wrong … Chase suppressed a shudder. He thought of the sexual predators whose names were being pulled for him to visit. If he and Judd did not find Steven within 48 hours, the chances of his being alive were … *No.* He would not be overcome with fear.

Lord, You're all knowing. All powerful. Help me find that little boy.

"I have the name for you," he heard from behind.

Chase turned to face Nadine. She had a stack of papers in her hands.

"Melanie Benson," Nadine said.

Upon hearing that name, Chase's heart skipped a beat. His wiped his palms on his pants. "Melanie Benson?" he asked for confirmation.

"Yes and my husband met with her just yesterday morning." Nadine pinned her eyes on him. "I lied to you earlier but I was ashamed. Francis and I were having serious problems and *she* was one of them."

Chase's knees weakened. "What do you mean?" He had to ask but he did not want to know. A sinking feeling settled in the pit of his stomach.

"Francis was having an affair. With Melanie Benson."

5

"Now I definitely have to see this Melanie Benson," Judd said as soon as they left the Ashton's home.

Their feet crunched on the gravel driveway.

Chase glared. "Your sense of humor is inappropriate. I'm sure there's an explanation."

Judd laughed. "I can't believe it. You're smitten. You saw this Melanie person for ten minutes and now you're her defender."

"I'm not her defender but I'm a good judge of character," Chase said. "Maybe there's another woman named Melanie Benson."

"Who works in a bank?"

Chase entered the police car on the passenger side and slammed the door. They were going back to the station for Chase to retrieve his car. He was going to question Melanie and Judd was going to investigate the sexual offenders in the neighborhood. Then they would meet back at the Ashton's to interrogate Francis. He was back out with the search party.

Judd entered the driver's side.

Chase continued the conversation. "Melanie Benson doesn't have a single blot on her license. She's a model citizen."

"How would you know that?"

Chase lifted his chin. "I …"

"You searched her background?"

Chase hemmed and hawed.

"Remind me to tease you about that later," Judd said, before continuing. "Melanie's license may be clean but it doesn't mean she didn't have an affair. You've been in this job long enough to know nothing is ever as it seems," Judd said. "You can't swear for anyone's innocence. You need cold, hard facts."

When they stopped at a light, Judd pulled a pack of gum out of his shirt pocket. He offered one to Chase before taking one for himself.

"Thanks." Chase undid the wrapper and popped the gum in his mouth. "I'm willing to bet on Francis Ashton's guilt. He's behind Steven's disappearance."

Judd pressed the accelerator. "On that we agree. Francis is wasting taxpayer's money and time with this search." He swung a glance Chase's way. "You know what I was thinking though. *How coincidental* that a deaf child disappears and his mother implicates a *deaf* investment banker."

"That's the only thing that has me …" No. Melanie would not do this. Chase looked out the window. He did not understand how he could be sure of someone he just met. But in his line of work, there was no such thing as coincidence.

Judd patted his arm. "I can interview Melanie if you'd like."

Chase shook his head. "No, I have to. I have to see her face ..."

For once Judd kept his smart comeback to himself. "I understand. I know I've been at you to start dating again after Simone but I didn't think you'd jump right into love."

"Let's not talk about Simone. She was a two-timing..." Chase stopped before he called Simone Norris a derogatory name.

He and Simone had been college sweethearts. Chase was all set to marry her when he finished the police academy. However, Simone was pregnant with another man's child by that time. Never mind that man had been one of his best friends. "I admit I felt an instant connection when I met Melanie, but I'm not in love. I don't know her."

Chase did not add that he had spent the entire weekend with Melanie on his mind. He had even prayed asking God for a chance to see her again. Well, God has a way of answering prayers.

Judd put on the flashing lights and increased his speed. "Okay, love is a strong word but remember when you meet with her, you're there on police business. Keep it professional."

Chase nodded, knowing Judd's advice was on point. Still, his heart rate increased and his stomach rumbled with nervous anticipation at the prospect of seeing Melanie. Pity it was because she was a potential suspect in a missing child's case.

"Are you going to bring your dad in on this case?" Judd asked, just before they parted ways.

Chase nodded. His father, the legendary Lieutenant Ted Lawson, had retired from the police force after thirty years on the job. Chase sometimes sought his expertise.

"Give him my regards." Judd headed into the precinct to pull the sex offender files.

Chase sent his father a text. UP TO A VISIT LATER?

Ted was retired but would be a cop until the day he died. He had probably seen this case on the news. Sure enough Chase's phone vibrated.

COME ON. CAUGHT SOME FISH THIS MORNING.

I'LL BE LATE, Chase texted back.

I'LL BE UP.

Chase placed his cell phone into his pants pocket. Thinking about Ted, Chase shook his head. Three years ago, on August 12, Chase lost his mother and brother in a car accident. He and Ted's relationship had been … *strained* since Ted had been the driver of the car. He had been driving drunk. Losing his wife and child must have been Ted's rock-bottom moment. He gave his life to God. It took months before Chase believed his father's transformation. Ted's conversion was proof God did exist. Things changed after that. Slowly, Chase and his father rebuilt their relationship. The following year, Chase gave his life to God.

Two years and counting and he never regretted his decision to put his life in God's hands. Talk about God turning things for His good.

Ten minutes later, Chase pulled mini mall and parked in front of the Wells Fargo bank. He glanced at his watch. It was close to 4:00 p.m.

Chase entered the bank. A young, blond-haired woman approached. "Can I help you?"

His tongue refused to cooperate. He was nervous to see her though he had a valid reason. Chase reminded himself he was on duty, not a date. "I'm here to see Melanie Benson."

"Melanie took a personal day. I'm Rachel Morrison, her best friend." The woman held out her hand. She studied him with obvious interest.

Chase returned the handshake and gave Rachel the once over. In her form-fitting red dress and black pumps, Rachel was stunning. But, his interest speedometer remained idle. "Do you have any idea where Melanie might be?" *She could be at home babysitting a 5-year-old.* Chase rebuked that thought.

"Knowing Melanie, she's probably at the Guys and Dolls dance studio in North Port, off 41," Rachel said. "It's right before you get to the Wal-Mart."

Chase's brows furrowed. "Dance studio?"

"Yes, Melanie went to her father's doctor's appointment today. Mr. Benson had a major heart attack six years ago. Dancing is her stress reliever. She almost always head there after her father's checkup." Rachel rattled on. "Melanie auditioned for *So You Think You Can Dance*. She wowed the judges. She could have gone to Juilliard but then her father …" She stopped as if realizing she was talking to a cop. Rachel twisted her hands. "Is Melanie in some trouble?"

51

He shook his head. "I have to ask her some questions about a case."

Rachel's eyebrows shot up. "Oh, I thought you were the police officer Melanie met on Friday ..." She stopped. "I'm rambling. I need to shut up."

Chase puffed his chest. Had Melanie talked about him? If so, that was promising.

He kept his tone neutral. "Thank you for your time. I'll head to the studio first." Within minutes he was on his way to the dance studio. A deaf person who danced. This he had to see.

The more he learned about her, the more intriguing Melanie became. Chase drove the short distance wondering how he would feel once he saw her. Maybe he had imagined the spark on their first meeting. He parked next to the grey Infiniti. There was only one way to find out.

Chase entered the studio. To his surprise, no one was there. He crooked his head and listened. There was music playing in the back room. Chase followed the sound until he stood by the door of one of the rooms. He scanned the polished wooden floors and the long iron bar. But Chase was mesmerized by the vision in the corner of the room.

Melanie wore a white leotard that framed her skin like a second glove. She had on white open-footed tights and a white airy skirt that stopped above her knees. To Chase, she looked like a nymph. Melanie was in the far corner. Her back was turned to him so she had not spotted him. Chase was glad to feast on her.

Melanie bent over to press the play button on her

MacBook Pro. She turned up the speakers attached to her laptop. Chase heard Chris Brown's and Jordin Sparks' *No Air* begin to play. Melanie stood with her arms above her head with her face lifted to the ceiling.

He wondered if she intended to move. Then Melanie swung into motion. She pointed a leg high into the air. Then she arched her body backwards. Chase saw her eyes were closed. She swooped her arms and contorted her body in different poses.

Though he was no expert, Chase could understand all she was saying through dance. With her hair pinned up, Chase could see the myriad of emotions outlined across Melanie's face in painstaking detail. Her quick, fluid movements showed fear, hope, and a yearning for... something.

Was she searching for me? Chase's heart tripped at the question.

Chase kept his eyes pinned on Melanie as she floated across the room. He felt every nuance, and every synchronized action she made elicited a stark response. Chase felt a tear brim his eye.

Near the end of the song, Melanie leapt into the air, landed on her feet, and spun around. She reminded him of the ballerina on a music box. Chase pulled out his cell phone to snap a picture. Melanie curled her body to the floor into a fetal position.

Chase clapped. He knew she could not hear, but he could not help his response. It was evident Melanie was meant to dance.

Chase's feet took him to where she lay. His shadow fell across the floor and Melanie's head popped up. Her eyes widened. Her body heaved but she kept her gaze on his, challenging him, weaving her magic, drawing him in. Chase slid closer. When he was in her personal space, he held out his hand.

Melanie clasped her smaller hand in his. Chase tugged her to her feet. She let out a gasp. Seeing her plush lips formed in a perfect 'O' Chase pulled her to him and crushed his lips to hers.

6

Melanie's arm circled Chase's waist as he deepened the kiss. When she had been dancing, Chase filled her mind. She had thought about him all weekend long. Then when she opened her eyes and saw him standing there with those compelling green eyes, Melanie had not been able to stop staring. She had never felt such a strong attraction to someone she just met. It was scary. But thrilling.

Chase slid his hand up her spine to caress the curls by her nape. She moaned as heat warmed her body. Instantly Chase broke the kiss. Melanie felt the loss and touched her lips.

Melanie ducked her head to hide her embarrassment. She had no idea if her moan turned him off. How did she know how she sounded?

Chase lifted her chin. "I had to stop before I lose control."

Melanie's heart warmed. "I thought I sounded funny and turned you off or something."

He shook his head. "No. You sounded ... sexy and your voice did things to my insides. I could barely breathe."

Melanie bit back a smile. "Oh."

"Yes. Oh." Chase ran his hands through his buzz cut. "For the first time in my life, I am in trouble of keeping on the straight and narrow, so to speak. Since I gave my life to God three years ago, I've been … I've held up."

She batted her lashes. "I'm a Christian, too. I've been going to church since I was five years old."

"You don't kiss like a good girl."

Melanie saw Chase's grin and knew he was teasing her. She twirled her foot in perfect figure 8s. "I am a good girl. Good at everything I do."

Chase's eyes darkened as her words sunk in. "Next time you dance, I want to dance with you," he said. He reached out to cup her face with his hands. His eyes held promise.

"It's a date," she breathed out.

He gave a slight shake of the head. "I came here to ask you some questions—official business—not to jump on you."

She knew her cheeks were a warm pink. Then Chase's words registered. "Official business?" Suddenly she felt cold. She rubbed her arms.

"I have a case and your name come up."

"I thought you wanted to see me, but you only sought me out because of your job," Melanie whispered. Could she be any less mortified? Wait a minute. What kind of official business would Chase have with her? She felt a light tap on her arm and bravely met Chase's gaze.

"Even if it weren't for this case, I would have

sought you out. I would've concocted a plan to see you again."

Melanie felt inordinately pleased at his words. She cleared her throat. "What did you need to see me about?"

Chase slid his glance away. Then he looked her dead in the eyes. "Do you know Dr. Francis Ashton?"

"Yes, he's one of my clients. We know each other very well." She scrunched her nose. Why was he asking her about Francis?

"Well enough for his wife to accuse him of having an affair. With you."

Melanie's eyes widened. "You think I'm having an affair with Francis?" She pictured the tall, dark-haired surgeon with his hawk-like nose. He was handsome if you like the patriarchal look. But, Francis was so not her type.

Neither was Chase until a few days ago.

"His wife thinks that." Chase straightened. "Francis' son went missing this morning and there's a manhunt underway. It's been all over the news. I need to ask you some questions."

She touched her heart. She felt the thumping against her hand. Melanie knew Francis had a deaf son, but what did his disappearance have to do with her? She supposed she would find out.

"I didn't catch the news today. Haven't been home. Let me get out of these clothes and gather my things." Melanie charged into the dressing room and changed into jeans and a black sweater. Then she fetched her bag, laptop, and speakers.

Chase and Melanie departed the studio. She activated the alarm before locking up. Chase helped her into her car and commanded her to follow him. Melanie pulled out her cell phone to text her parents.

She saw several text messages from Rachel and Tricia. They said Chase was looking for her and were worried.

She sent them a group text: ON MY WAY WITH CHASE NOW. LET'S MEET UP LATER.

Melanie followed Chase and was surprised when he pulled into the Perkin's parking lot. They entered the restaurant and chose a booth in the back. Melanie ordered the chicken fried steak with potatoes and Chase ordered the turkey dinner. They both chose lemonades.

Chase took out his notepad. "Tell me about your relationship with Francis Ashton."

Melanie scrunched her nose at his use of the word, 'relationship.'

"Francis has banked with Wells Fargo for over twelve years. I've been his chief financial adviser for three years. Francis accumulated a lot of cash through his 401Ks. Two years ago, he made an appointment to see me. He said he wanted to invest his money, secure his son's future. At first he kept it safe. Against my advice, Francis put his money into some crazy ventures. He suffered a heavy financial loss. He can recoup his funds but it will take time."

Chase perked up. "What time did you see him Monday morning?"

Melanie pulled up the calendar on her phone. "It was 8:15, to be exact. We met for an hour. When he left, he was crushed. To lose one hundred thousand dollars overnight is a huge blow for anyone. Francis confided he had taken out a loan without my knowledge. He purchased a condo somewhere here in town and made some more extravagant purchases. He put his business and home up for collateral. If he defaults ..."

Chase's eyes widened. That was some serious money. And motive. Motive to fake your son's kidnapping to get your wife's money.

"What about Nadine's interests? Do you oversee hers as well?"

Melanie shook her head. "Not anymore. Nadine comes from old money. Her parents hold the purse strings but she has done well with her own investments. No matter what happens to Francis, Nadine will be all right. Steven is her sole beneficiary. Francis resented that."

Chase rubbed his chin. Nadine mentioned her parents were putting up one hundred grand. But, from the look of things, Francis needed more.

"Did you ever meet with Francis outside of work?"

Melanie nodded. "All the time. Francis worked long hours. He would take me to dinner and we would discuss his investments."

"Does your boss approve of your late night meetings?" Chase hated the image of Melanie out to dinner with anybody but him. He was surprised at his possessiveness.

She nodded. "Yes, it's done. Business dinners are tax deductible and Francis made us serious money."

Chase leaned in closer. "If it's all business, why does his wife think you're having an affair?"

Melanie squirmed. "I don't know."

"Can I see you again?"

Chase's question caught her off guard. "You want to go out with me? Like on a date? Can you do that?" She tilted her head.

"I admit I've never dated a person that's a part of my investigation but I have to see you. I don't want to sound like a stalker, but now that I've met you, I can't let you go. It'll be complicated but I'm willing to try if you'll give me a chance. We can keep our personal lives separate from the case."

Their food arrived. Melanie was glad for the reprieve. This conversation was intense. What frightened her was that she was considering Chase's proposal. Melanie cut into her steak. "This smells heavenly."

Chase put another piece of turkey into his mouth. "Hmm, tastes just as good, too."

"I need to know something. I know you had to ask but do you think I slept with a married man?"

He stared. "No, I don't. But I admit I considered it briefly. The same day Steven, who's deaf, goes missing, you take a personal day."

Melanie felt a chill. She understood Chase's thought pattern. "I was with my father. He had to get his yearly physical."

"I know," he said. "Your friend, Rachel, told me." Chase waved his fork. "And, for the record, I don't think you're involved in Steven's disappearance."

She wrinkled her nose. "But you think Francis is behind it, don't you?"

"I can't answer that," Chase said.

Melanie sipped her lemonade. "I see. Does that fall under," she formed quotes with her fingers, "official police business?"

He nodded. Then Chase pushed his plate toward her and jumped into the booth next to her. Their legs touched. Melanie liked the warmth of Chase's muscled legs against hers. He held her hand and touched her face. Melanie faced him.

"This is not police business now, by the way," Chase said.

"I should hope not," Melanie replied.

The two chatted and laughed throughout their meal. The intensity between them grew. Melanie felt as if she had known Chase for years instead of days.

Melanie fed Chase the last piece of her steak. She watched his mouth slide off her spoon. Desire rippled through her being. Melanie sought to distract herself. "So what church do you attend?"

"I attend New Life Seventh Day Church when I can. Pastor Woodson's sermons always teach me something new. I hate to miss services, but sometimes duty calls." Chase looked at his watch. "Speaking of which, I have to meet my partner, Judd. We're questioning Francis."

Melanie swallowed her disappointment and looked at her watch. "It's fine. I have to meet with Rachel and Tricia anyway."

Chase smacked her on the lips. "I don't know when I'll have a free night. Finding Steven is top priority." He crooked his head. "Do you have any vacation time?"

Melanie squinted her eyes. "I do. Why?"

"I wanted to know if you'd be interested in tagging along with me the next couple of days. It might not come to that because I think I can crack this case. But, Steven is deaf and since you know sign language, you can help me communicate with him if—no, when—we find him."

"That's a bit unorthodox," she said.

"It is, but nothing since I've met you has been ordinary. I think God made me meet you last Friday. I was meant to pull you over that day." He wiped his mouth and settled the bill. "Let me know." He gave her his contact information.

Melanie had never done anything so adventurous. The idea of riding around in a police car thrilled her. Truth be told, she would venture into a pig's sty with Chase. He was that intriguing.

"I'll think about it," she said. Melanie scribbled her cell phone number and FaceTime email address on the back of her business card and handed it to Chase.

"Can I call you?"

"Yes, but s lips, I use FaceTime. If you call my cell, you can leave always leave a message. A relay service transcribes my voicemail for me. But I prefer texting like most of our generation, because it's so much easier and faster, " Melanie said with a smile.

"Cool. I'll catch up with you later." Chase pushed her card into his pants pocket and rushed out the restaurant.

Melanie sat toying with the straw in her glass and recounted every moment with Chase. She touched her lips remembering his sultry kisses. Her mind liked him. Her body liked him. Her spirit liked him. She exhaled. Her heart was somersaulting into love.

7

"This has been one never-ending day. So far, two of the perps panned out. I'm going to see the third tomorrow." Judd yawned loud enough to rival an elephant in the jungle. It was close to 9:00 p.m. Chase and Judd stood outside the Ashton's home. The house was littered with cops and volunteers.

"After talking with Melanie, I think we can crack Francis. Get him to fess up. Steven should be home by midnight," Chase said with confidence.

Judd opened his mouth, but Chase held a hand up. "No negativity. We're heading toward 24 hours since Steven is missing and I know what that could mean. I refuse to believe it. Steven is alive and well."

Judd closed his mouth and rang the doorbell. Selena greeted them and ushered them back to the kitchen.

"I'll get Mrs. Ashton. She's beside herself with worry and took to her bed. Her parents are with her," Selena said.

"Nadine's in bed?" Judd's voice caught.

Chase furrowed his brow. His friend was usually unruffled. He grasped Judd's arm and read the stark fear in his eyes. "Judd?"

Judd shook his head. "I'm all right. Hearing about

Nadine ..."

Chase's eyes widened. "You like her," he whispered.

"No, I'm concerned about a worried mother," Judd replied, sounding more like himself. Chase held back his retort.

Nadine came into view. Gone was the sharp woman from the morning. Her hair was disheveled and he could see she had spent the day crying.

"Any word?" she croaked out, rubbing her temples. She clutched Steven's picture in one hand.

Judd stepped toward Nadine before appearing to catch himself. Chase looked at Judd's jutted jaw and knew his friend was denying his attraction. Hmmm.... Chase would find a way to rib him about it later.

A distinguished older couple, whom Chase assumed were Nadine's parents, entered the room. Chase took in their designer outfits. Not a hair was out of place. They smelled of money.

The gentleman extended his hand. "I'm Peter Goodman and this is Marie."

Both Chase and Judd shook his hand.

"Nadine told us to hold off on the ransom money but we're worried about our grandson. Money loosens the tongue. We'd like to put our offer out there tomorrow," Peter said.

"I understand your need to do something. But Judd and I have a hunch. Give us until the 24 hour mark," Chase said.

Nadine wailed. "Oh, no. If we don't find Steven

tonight …" She dissolved into tears. Marie made a move toward her but Judd beat her to it. He enfolded Nadine in his arms and led her over to the couch. Her body shook with tears.

She lifted tear-streaked lashes to Judd. "Please tell me you'll find him."

"We will," Judd assured her. Nadine buried her head into his chest.

Peter's eyes narrowed and Marie pursed her lips at the intimate scene.

Chase intervened. "Is Francis around? Judd and I came back to speak with him." Chase gave Judd a pointed stare. He had yet to loosen his hold on Nadine. Judd shrugged, returning Chase's stare.

"Francis is in his office. He came in to shower about an hour ago. He's expecting you," Peter said.

"I'll go get him," Marie volunteered. She swept out of the room with a regal lift of her chin.

"Nadine, would you like some tea?" Peter asked.

Nadine lifted her head and extricated herself from Judd's arms. "Yes, Dad. My head is pounding."

To Chase, Peter looked relieved she had broken contact with Judd. Peter held out a hand to his daughter. With the delicacy of fine china, Nadine placed her hand in her father's. He ushered her out of the room.

"What are you doing?" Chase asked Judd once they were alone.

"I … Nadine is in pain. What do you want me to

do?" Judd sauntered over to Chase's side without an apologetic bone in his body.

Chase dropped the argument. "Let's take Francis into the station. Riding in the backseat of a police car should shake him up."

"Good idea." Judd smiled. "He can ride with me."

Francis strolled into the room wearing an oversized green sweater, black jeans, and black loafers.

"Let's go," Judd said. He slapped a pair of handcuffs onto Francis's hands none too gently.

"Is all this necessary?" Francis panicked. "I am willing to answer any questions. You didn't need to do this to me."

"We're taking you down to the precinct for questioning," Chase said, giving Judd a quelling glare. Judd was enjoying this a bit too much.

"Am I under arrest?" Francis squeaked like a mouse in a trap.

"No, but that's subject to change. Depending on what you tell us," Judd said. He tugged on the cuffs to lead Francis out of the house.

Nadine and her parents were back in the room by then.

"What's going on?" Nadine's face paled.

"We're taking Francis into custody."

"Should we secure an attorney?" Peter asked.

"Not necessary, but it's your right," Chase said. "We believe Francis knows more about Steven's disappearance than he's letting on and we intend to find out." He pivoted and strode to the door.

Judd shoved Francis into the back of his patrol car and sped off. Francis lowered his head until his chin touched his chest. Chase would have felt sorry for the other man if a child's life was not at stake.

Chase got into his vehicle. He pulled out Melanie's card, admiring her penmanship. He missed her already. He pressed the FaceTime app on his iPhone and plugged her email address into his cell phone, then pressed DIAL. Melanie's face popped up on his screen.

"Are you home?" he asked.

"Not yet," she said. "I'm stopping by my friend Rachel's condo first."

"I'll be at the station late, so I will catch up with you tomorrow."

"Okay," Melanie said. "I'll take the time off if you need it."

Chase smiled. "If things work out right, you won't need to."

"I'm hoping for that as well."

Chase ended the call before he spouted how much he missed her. It was too soon for those declarations and he did not want to scare her off. He turned on the engine and put the car in gear. He could not wait for this case to end so he could focus his energies on more pleasant past times. Like Melanie.

Francis was already in the interview room when Chase arrived. He slipped into the seat next to Judd. Chase retrieved his notepad from his shirt pocket.

"Tell us about your investments," Chase began.

Francis licked his lips. "Can I have some water?" he asked.

Both Chase and Judd recognized Francis' stalling for what it is, but Judd complied with his wishes. He slammed the small cup of water in front of Francis.

"Start talking," Judd commanded.

"I made a few poor choices and thought the answer was to take out a loan." Francis slid back in his chair. He shuddered. "Bad idea. Nadine and I had a fight about it this morning. Actually, we have been fighting for the past few months."

Chase was not fooled by Francis's conciliatory attitude. He knew the type. Francis thought that by being agreeable and cooperative, he could outsmart them. Throw them off his scent.

"Is that all you and Nadine fought about?" Judd asked.

Francis had the grace to look ashamed. "I suppose she told you she *thinks* I'm having an affair." His scoffing tone grated on Chase's nerves.

"Are you?" Chase pinned him with a gaze.

Francis drummed his fingers on the table. Then he lowered his voice. "Man to man? I dipped out here and there but it was nothing serious."

Chase's heart rate increased. Did he dip out with Melanie? "Nadine felt you were seeing your investment banker."

Francis squirmed. "Melanie?" He shook his head.

"Melanie's a great girl, smart as a whip, but she's not ..." He stole a furtive glance at Judd before lifting his chin. "I don't date outside my race."

Wow. Chase let that comment slide but he wanted to slap Francis into the present century. Francis was a weasel. Chase was glad to hear Francis had not been with *his* Melanie.

Your Melanie?

"So if you weren't with Melanie, who were you with?" Judd asked, bringing Chase out of his musings.

Francis smirked. "Do you need a list?"

Judd shot out the chair and grabbed Francis by the collar. "Listen you smart a—"

"Judd, no," Chase yelled.

Judd snarled into Francis' face with the control of a raging bull.

"Let him go," Chase commanded.

With a grunt, Judd dropped Francis into the chair before he left the room.

"What's his problem?" Francis adjusted his clothes. "I don't like being treated like an animal."

Chase was done with this joker. He looked Francis directly in the eyes. "Where is Steven?"

"I don't know where my son is. If I knew, I wouldn't be out there searching for him."

"You do know where Steven is. You set this whole kidnapping up because you want your hands on Nadine's money. How convenient that the day you learn you lose one hundred grand, your in-laws are offering that same amount for Steven's safe return. What do you plan to do to get the rest of the money you need?"

Francis hemmed and hawed. "I would *never* harm my son."

"You call putting his mother through terror not harming your son?" Chase pushed. He was going to hammer at Francis until he cracked.

"I ... I ... only wanted ..." Francis trailed off.

"What did you want?" Chase zoned in. "You wanted money? Never mind that your son is probably crying his eyes out, hungry and alone."

Francis flinched. "No! Steven is fine!" His eyes widened when he realized what he had said. Francis amended his words. "I—I've got to believe that."

"How can you be sure? There are three pedophiles in a 20-mile radius. One of them we are unable to find."

Francis bunched his fists. Sweat formed on his forehead. He took a swig of his water. "I'll tell you everything."

Jackpot.

Chase slammed his hand on the small table. "Start from the beginning."

Judd re-entered the room.

Francis told Chase about his financial struggles, confirming Melanie's statement. Francis added he was in danger of losing his practice. Chase understood Francis' panic but that would not excuse his

71

reprehensible actions. Chase asked, "Where is Steven?"

Francis's shoulders slumped. "I was in the backyard and I saw when Nadine left for the bathroom. It was spur of the moment. I closed my office and left him there until I could get him. Then I ditched the search party and doubled back to drop him off to my girlfriend's home. No one noticed I was missing."

"You left a minor on his own for hours?" Chase asked.

"Girlfriend?" Judd blinked.

Francis nodded yes to both questions. "Yes. Her name is Rachel Morrison and we've been together for about ten months. Rachel has him. Steven's safe at her place."

Rachel Morrison? Chase furrowed his brows. He wondered why that name sounded so familiar. Rachel ... Rachel ...

"Where did you meet Rachel?" Judd spat out.

"She works at Wells Fargo."

"We'll call off the manhunt and alert the press." Judd slapped handcuffs on Francis to take him for booking. He recited the Miranda rights and Francis asked for his attorney.

Melanie's friend. Chase remembered the cool blonde from earlier. Melanie and Rachel were close friends. Melanie must have known about Francis and Rachel. Maybe she was covering for them.

He flashed to his earlier conversation and his heart sunk. Melanie had told him she was going to Rachel's home. To check in on Steven? Or, to warn her friend?

Chase could not be sure.

But he was going to find out.

8

Melanie had lied to Chase. It was a lie by omission but a lie nonetheless. She knew who had prepared Francis' loan.

Melanie stood outside Rachel's second floor two-bedroom condo and pressed the doorbell. "Rachel, open up. I know you're in there. I saw your car."

Melanie rapped the door. "If you don't answer, I'll use the spare key." She bent over to lift the mat.

The door opened a crack. Rachel peered through the small slit. "I can't talk now, Melanie. I—I'm not well. Come by tomorrow."

Melanie stood. "I *must* speak to you." When it seemed as if Rachel hesitated, Melanie pressed her body against the door. She had to confront her friend.

Rachel had no choice but to let her inside.

Melanie scanned the living area. She eyed the tangerine painted walls with white trimmings and the chic-designed orange and brown-checkered sofa and chaise. Her eyes roamed over the delicate art pieces on the walls and the sculptures Rachel had collected through the years. Melanie heaved a sigh of relief. She had not known what she expected to see but nothing was amiss.

She addressed Rachel, who wore *Victoria Secret Pink* pajamas. "You look *well*."

Rachel's hands hung at her sides. "I'm sorry I lied. I needed to be alone."

Melanie sniffed the air. "Did you make popcorn?"

"Yes. I suddenly had a taste for it."

Melanie squinted her eyes. She moved into Rachel's space. "But you hate popcorn. Ever since you almost choked on a kernel, you avoid it like the plague."

"I felt for it. Can we just leave it at that? I'm grown. I'm allowed to change my mind. What is this, the third degree?"

Melanie was shocked at the edge in Rachel's voice. Rachel was being snappy and that was so unlike her.

"I find it odd, that's all." Melanie dropped her Dolce & Gabbana leather purse on the cream-colored tile. "I think the cops are going to come looking for you."

Rachel's face whitened. "For what?"

"Chase questioned me today about Dr. Francis Ashton." Melanie kept her gaze pinned on Rachel's face for some reaction. She continued, "His son went missing today."

Rachel nodded. "Yes, it's been all over the news. It's such a shame." The blond strolled into the kitchenette and busied herself by wiping the marble counters.

That was a dead giveaway. Any time Rachel was nervous, she started cleaning. Melanie walked over to her and tapped her on the arm.

"His wife thinks Francis and I are involved."

"Say what?" Rachel dropped the cloth.

"Of course, I set Chase straight about me and Francis. We're business associates. Nothing more." Melanie hoped Rachel would fess up but her friend was cool.

"Glad you did that. You would never give Francis the time of day."

"But, you would," Melanie challenged.

Rachel put distance between them. She squared her shoulders. "I—It happened once. I slept with him one time and then I ended it. I couldn't handle the guilt," she said. Rachel bowed her head.

Melanie ambled over to her friend. She used her finger to tuck Rachel's chin and tilted Rachel's head towards her. "You bought this fancy condo," Melanie signed back. "Did Francis help you buy it after *one* time?"

"Fine!" Rachel flailed her arms. "The truth is we've been dating for ten months. Francis gave me the thirty thousand as a down payment on the condo. I was ashamed to tell you."

Melanie's eyes widened. "Ten months. You dated a married man for ten months and you didn't tell your friends?"

"I knew what you and Tricia would say. I'm not like you. I ... I need someone." Rachel twisted her hands.

"But you also took money from him? He has a wife

and son at home. Does that mean nothing to you?"

Rachel eyes filled with tears. "I wasn't thinking. I'm in love with him."

Melanie shook Rachel's shoulders. "You can't be serious. Francis Ashton kidnapped his son. How can you love a man who would put his own child in danger?"

"Steven's not in danger," Rachel said. "I know that."

Melanie narrowed her eyes. "How do you know that? Rachel, in the space of ten minutes, you've lied to me twice. Please tell me the truth."

"Francis took him! He told me earlier. That's how I know."

After Rachel dropped that news, Melanie rushed into the living room. She picked up her purse and dug around for her phone. "You slept with a married man but that doesn't make you an accessory. You'll be painted as a home wrecker but that's not punishable by law. But, Rachel you have to go to the cops. There's a massive manhunt and people are combing the forests when Steven is all right. Let me call Chase. He'll know what to do."

Rachel waved her hands to get Melanie's attention. "No. No, you can't do that." She chewed her bottom lip. "Let me think and figure this out."

"What's there to figure out?" Melanie found her cell phone.

Rachel rushed over and snatched the phone out of Melanie's hand. "Since you can't leave well enough alone, come with me." Rachel gripped Melanie's wrist with surprising force and tugged her toward the master bedroom.

Rachel's king-sized bed was made and there were ten pillows artfully arranged on the eyelet comforter. But, Melanie's eyes were trained on the toys on the bed. She noticed flashing images on Rachel's television screen. It was on the cartoon channel and the subtitles were on.

Toys were on Rachel's bed. Subtitles on. That could only mean one thing.

Melanie shook her head. "No. Don't tell me. Please don't tell me you have Steven here."

Rachel nodded. "Francis dropped him here when I got in from work. I couldn't say no. Steven's grandparents are going to pay a huge ransom for his return. A ransom I plan to collect for me and Francis."

"Rachel, you're out of your mind if you think you can get away with this," Melanie said. "Give me my phone. I'm telling you, Chase will go easy on you."

"I can get away with it, and I will."

"Where is Steven?" Melanie gritted out. "I'll take him home. Just give him to me. I promise I won't implicate you."

Rachel appeared to consider Melanie's words. "Fine. I'll give him to you."

Melanie hugged her. "You're doing the right thing."

Rachel looked doubtful but she pointed toward the closet. "Steven's in there."

Melanie's heart pounded in her chest. "You locked him in the closet? Who are you? Right now I feel as if I don't know you."

She slowly made her way to Rachel's walk-in closet and peered inside. She could not see anything. Melanie turned on the light switch but the bulb must have blown. Melanie battled claustrophobia but she crept further into the space. She needed to get to Steven. Melanie thought she saw his feet underneath Rachel's dresses. She stooped down.

Her hair blew from a sudden gush of wind. The door hit Melanie on the butt. She stumbled but did not fall.

Melanie swung around but Rachel had quicker reflexes. Rachel was on the other side of the door pushing it close. Melanie pushed back. "Quit playing. Let me out of here."

Rachel stuck her head through the crack. "I'll take your phone with me. Can't have you calling your cop friend."

"Let me out!" Melanie screamed.

"I'm sorry," Rachel mouthed and slammed the door shut.

"No!" Melanie scrambled to her feet. She wiggled the lock.

She pushed against the door with all her might but she was stuck. *No. Please, God, no.* Hysteria set in. Melanie pounded on the door. "Don't lock me in here. Rachel let me out! I can't be in here. Rachel! Rachel! Please. Help me! Let me out!"

9

"If that isn't a Kodak moment, I don't know what is." Chase pointed toward the woman and child vacating the second floor condo. It was dark but he knew that bleach blonde hair anywhere. Her back was turned and she was locking her front door. He crept into the parking lot.

Most of the residents were home and the lot was silent. *Perfect.*

Judd whistled. "It can't be this easy."

Chase laughed. "Sometimes it is. Unless my eyes are deceiving me, that is Rachel Morrison holding Steven Ashton's hand."

"And, she has a duffel bag and her purse," Judd said. "Looks like we came just in time."

Chase swerved the patrol car and parked directly behind Rachel's Ford Bronco to block her in. The realization that if he had pulled in a minute later he would have missed her, hit him. Chase knew it was perfect timing set up by a perfect God. He turned the headlights off. By Rachel's unhurried stride, she had not spotted them. She had not thought to look down into the parking lot or she would have seen them.

A sign of her confidence. Or stupidity.

"Let's do this," Judd said. He jogged over to the staircase, hiding in the shadows.

"Thank you, Lord," Chase whispered before exiting the vehicle.

As a habit, Chase tapped his gun at his side then felt the side of his belt buckle for his mace. He stood across from Judd who would give the signal.

As soon as Rachel hit the last stair, Judd nodded. Chase jumped out of the shadows. He grabbed Rachel and Judd grabbed Steven.

"Rachel Morrison, you're under arrest ..." Chase read Rachel the Miranda Rights and led her to the patrol car. Besides a sharp intake of breath, Rachel surrendered without a fight.

He looked behind briefly to see Judd hoist Steven in his arms and grab Rachel's duffel bag.

Both men walked with their chests puffed out. They were both glad and relieved for the outcome in this case. It would feel good to ring the doorbell and see a mother reunited with her son.

Chase smiled. These are the days he loved his job.

"C'mon little man. You're going home," Judd said.

"You do know he can't hear you," Chase pointed out. He opened the rear door and put Rachel inside. She rolled her eyes.

Judd bounced Steven in his arms. The little boy laughed. "I know he can't hear but I feel he understands. Right little guy?"

Steven rested his head on Judd's shoulders. Chase

chuckled.

Judd sat Steven in the front seat between them.

Chase patted Steven's arm. The little boy smiled at him. His missing teeth made Chase's heart melt.

Judd called into the station to relay the good news and to call off the manhunt. Chase sped through the deserted streets. Getting Steven home was their top priority. Rachel Morrison could rot for all he cared.

Melanie crossed Chase's mind. He would send her a text to let her know the good news.

By the time Chase pulled into the Ashton's property, Steven was asleep and drooling on Judd's leg.

"Poor little fellow. He's had an eventful day," Judd said.

Rachel still had not uttered a single word. She had not even shed a tear. Yet. But, she would.

Chase had not put the gear fully in park when Judd opened the door. He scooped Steven into his arms.

The front door flew open. Nadine scurried toward them with her arms opened wide. "Steven! Steven!" she yelled.

Judd shook Steven awake. When the youngster spotted his mom, he squirmed. He stretched his arms out and kicked his legs. Judd had to put him down. Steven moved like a tornado and catapulted into his mother's arms. Nadine twirled him around splattering his face with kisses. Chase, Judd, and the other officers present wiped their eyes.

Judd pumped a fist into the air.

"Good job," one of the officers said. A small applause broke out.

Nadine broke away from Steven to give Judd a tight squeeze. Chase was taken aback by her show of emotion. Judd hugged her tight basking in her thanks and praise.

"I had a hand in it too," he mumbled. Chase went to the patrol car to wait for Judd. Chase flashed the lights. He wanted to leave before Nadine spotted her husband's mistress in the backseat. At least Rachel had the good sense to crouch so she was hidden from view.

Chase's mind wandered to Melanie. He had forgotten to text her. He would. As soon as he got to the station.

Judd walked over and peered inside. "I'll find my way back. I want to see Nadine settled."

Chase eyes widened. "Since when …" He shook his head but kept his thoughts to himself.

"Why did you do it?" he asked Rachel once he pulled away from the Ashton's residence.

Her lips poked. "I'm not talking to you. I want my phone call."

Chase shrugged. A phone call would not save her from jail time. She was an accomplice. Rachel and Francis would be behind bars for a long time. He turned on the radio. *Dare You to Move* by Switchfoot played on Joy 88.1 FM. Chase turned up the volume. He loved this song. Chase sang along to that and to the Newsboys' *God's Not Dead*. He praised until he arrived at the precinct.

Chase helped Rachel out the car and led her into the station. He rubbed his eyes. Lord, he was tired. He wanted Rachel booked and paperwork completed in record time. He yawned. Chase pictured his king-sized bed waiting for him at home.

Again the urge to text Melanie hit his brain. Okay, he would text her as soon as he delivered Rachel over to another officer. Someone else could take her statement. His bed was calling.

Unfortunately, it was a busy night for Charlotte County PD. Chase ushered Rachel into the interview room. He would get her confession and take her personal items during booking. There was a huge desk in the middle of the room with two chairs on each side. Chase undid Rachel's cuffs and pointed for her to take one of the chairs nearest to the wall. Rachel dropped in the chair and rubbed her wrists.

He took out his notepad and sat in one of the two chairs closest to the door. "Ready to talk?"

Rachel folded her arms. "Not without my attorney present. I need my phone call."

Chase gritted his teeth. "Sure. It's your right." His chair scraped the floor as he stood. He pointed to the phone on the side of the desk.

"Make your phone call. I'll be back." He left the room to use the restroom.

Call Melanie. The thought hit him hard. God was telling him to call her. Chase reached for his cell phone and pulled up Melanie's contact information. He pressed the CALL button. After a couple rings, it went to voicemail.

"Melanie, this is Chase. I'm at the precinct. I shouldn't say this but you'll hear it soon on the news anyway. We took your friend, Rachel, into custody. I'm going to be taking her statement and that could take all night," he said. "I'll call you in the morning."

Chase swiped the END button. The thought occurred that Melanie's relay service might take too long. Chase quickly composed a text message.

I'M AT THE PRECINCT. RACHEL IS IN CUSTODY. COULD BE HERE ALL NIGHT. CALL YOU TOMORROW.

Chase hit send, then slipped his cell phone into his pants pocket, and reentered the room.

"Skip Wilson will be here in ten minutes," Rachel said.

Chase resisted the urge to moan. Skip Wilson would have him here for days. With his purple and green suits and weird-colored ties, Skip looked like a clown. But, it was all for show. Skip was lethal and thorough.

Chase uttered a prayer. This case was cut and dry. He banked on Skip advising Rachel to let Francis take the fall. Skip would seek a plea deal for a lighter sentence. Chase believed Rachel would jump on it but that was for the prosecuting attorney to handle.

Right now, he needed Rachel's statement.

Chase took a seat. Rachel glared.

Call Melanie.

Chase furrowed his brow. *I did.* He pinned his gaze on Rachel. "Did you see Melanie today?"

Rachel's head bent into a nod before she shook her head. "I didn't see her."

Chase tilted his chair. "That's odd because Melanie told me she was going to your place." He tried to remember if he had seen Melanie's car in the parking lot. But he could not. Chase had been too focused on Rachel and Steven.

Rachel met his gaze. "She must have changed her mind because I didn't."

She was cool, this one.

"How long did Melanie stay? Did she know about Steven?"

"I said I didn't see Melanie." Rachel showed him the middle finger. "Do you need your hearing check? Should I sign it? I didn't see her."

Okay. She wanted to be hard. Chase jumped to his feet. He snatched her up and took her out into the hall. "How about I put you in holding?"

Rachel tripped over her feet. "If you don't let me go, I'll scream police brutality."

Rachel's threats did not bother him. Chase knew he was not hurting her. He tossed Rachel into the cell with two other regulars. One was Shaquanda, a prostitute who loved girls.

Shaquanda licked her lips. She jabbed Brandy, the huge redhead next to her, in the arm. "Look at the candy Officer Chase brought us."

Rachel dug her heels in. "Please no. Don't leave me in here." Her lips quivered.

Chase eyed her. "Did you see Melanie today?"

Rachel snuck a look at Shaquanda and Brandy. She looked back at Chase and nodded. He stifled a laugh. He could smell her fear.

Chase led Rachel back into the interrogation room. "No more stalling. Did Melanie know about Steven?"

"She showed up at my door even though I texted and told her not to come," Rachel said. She pushed her hand in her pocket. "I was shocked to hear her knocking on my door. And to answer your second question, Melanie didn't know about Steven. She didn't know about any of it." Rachel slumped. "I'm sorry. I don't know how I got caught up in any of this."

Chase knew Rachel was ready to talk.

Call Melanie interrupted his plan.

This time Chase obeyed. He pressed the CALL button. He crooked his ear. What was that sound? It sounded like … a vibration? His eyes narrowed.

Rachel's hand was in her pocket. Her face betrayed her. Chase held out his hand. She removed the phone and placed it in his palm.

Fear sliced through him followed by a rage unlike any he had ever known. Chase knees weakened but his voice was eerily controlled. "Rachel, why do you have Melanie's phone?"

10

"Yea, though I walk through the shadow ... Of the valley." Melanie trembled. She was curled on the floor with her hands covering her face. *No, that was wrong.* "Though I walk through the valley of the shadow of death, I will fear no evil ..." Melanie shuddered. She had banged on the closet door until her hand bled. She screamed but no one heard her.

This was her fifth time repeating Psalm 23 and it was not helping.

"Oh, God. I'm going to die in here," Melanie cried. She had no idea how long she had been confined. Her hair was soaking wet from sweat and tears. Her throat felt scratchy. Sweat dripped from her face and trickled down her breasts. She used her shirt to dry off. "Why won't You help me?"

I am here.

Melanie sniffed. "I know but I'm scared."

She kicked her feet to bang on the door. "Help!" she screamed. "Somebody help me."

Help is on the way.

Melanie was too distraught to listen to His voice.

"Help! Help!" she screamed. How did she know if

her voice still worked? Melanie had screamed so much, she could be hoarse and not know it. Nevertheless, she grabbed a shoe and banged on the door.

She broke.

"Mama! Mama! Help me!" Melanie battled hysteria. Memories of another time plagued her mind. She swayed to the past. "God, this is too much. I can't ... I can't stay in here any longer. Uncle's going to beat me because I have to pee and I can't pee the floor."

She swayed to the present. "Rachel locked me in here. I was trying to help Steven ... I ... Lord, I ... Help me!"

Trust me.

The smell of camphor balls hit her nose. She felt closed in. She could not breathe. Tears slid down her cheeks. She used her hand to brush them away.

Trust me.

Melanie had no other choice.

She grabbed onto God's soothing voice. She opened her mouth, "I will lift up mine eyes to the hills from whence cometh my help. My help cometh from the Lord."

That's right. She did not need her Mama to help her. She did not need Rachel. She had God. He was with her all along.

Melanie released short staccato breaths until her strength and sanity return. "He will not suffer my foot to be moved. He never slumbers nor sleeps. I will trust in You, Lord."

Help is on the way.

Melanie nodded. It had taken her hours but she got it. She slid to her knees and bowed her head to pray.

She felt a whoosh. For a minute she thought it was the Holy Ghost but then a beam of light fell across her feet. Melanie looked up into a pair of green eyes.

"Melanie."

She wobbled to her feet and fell into Chase's arms. She knew she looked a hot mess but she was too happy to care. Melanie released her fears and her chest heaved from the weight of her tears. She cried and cried welcoming the feel of Chase's strong arms.

He kissed her hair. He brushed her hair off her face and kissed her forehead. He kissed her cheeks. Then he found her mouth.

Hungry, Melanie welcomed the feel of Chase's lips on hers. She grabbed his head and deepened the kiss. She took on his strength until Chase tore his lips off hers.

"You found me," she said.

"God led me to you."

Melanie nodded. "I know He did. I was hysterical but He kept saying, 'Help is on the way.'"

"Hallelujah!"

"Rachel locked me in here," Melanie said. She touched her chest. "She has Steven."

Chase nodded. "I know. We caught her, and Steven is safe at home. Rachel told me what she did to you."

Melanie's heart ached for her friend. "She didn't mean it."

Chase eyes hardened. "Rachel's in her right mind. She knew what she was doing. We'll leave her in the hands of the court."

"I'll put her in God's hands," Melanie said.

Chase jutted his jaw. He held her hand and led her out of Rachel's condo. Melanie grabbed her purse. When she was by her vehicle, Chase handed Melanie her cell phone. Melanie saw text messages from Tricia and her parents. She sent them each a quick text saying she was okay.

"I'll follow you home," Chase said.

Melanie's knees buckled. "I can't ..."

Chase crooked his head. "Come with me. I'll take you home. Judd and I will get your car for you tomorrow."

"But what about work?" Melanie questioned.

"Take a day off." Chase secured her vehicle and Melanie was glad to let him be in charge.

"Thank you, Chase," she spoke and signed. Melanie's body melted against the seat. She was so tired she did not even know when she closed her eyes.

The next thing she knew, Chase was shaking her awake. Melanie opened her eyes.

"Where am I?" she signed.

Chase shook his head. Melanie used her voice to repeat the question.

"You're at my place. I didn't want to take you home when you've been tossing from nightmares."

"Nightmares?"

"Yes, you were groaning and mumbling Uncle or something."

Melanie stiffened. "That's from a long time ago." She tossed her hair and affected an "I don't care" attitude.

Chase did not look like he bought her act. He escorted her into his home. Her tired eyes scanned his place, noting its cleanliness, but she would not be able to recall the décor or the color of the paint on the wall.

"I have a spare bedroom. You can take a shower. I have an oatmeal body wash you can use. I'll get you one of my t-shirts." He meandered down a narrow hallway and opened the last door. He led her into a large guest room with light purple walls. The full-sized bed boasted coordinated linens and wall treatments. She felt at home.

Melanie held up her hand. "Can I get some Advil?"

Chase nodded.

He quickly returned with two of the gel caps and a glass of water. Melanie swallowed them hoping they would alleviate the pain in her hand. It sported a nasty purple bruise.

While he was gone, Melanie stripped down to her undies. She walked into the bathroom and turned on the shower. She tested the water and waited for it to heat up. Then she stepped inside. The heat pelted her skin and soothed her frayed nerves. Melanie washed her underwear and hung it to dry. She grabbed one of the large plush towels from the linen closet in the bathroom and walked the short path back to the bed.

Drying off, she spotted a white t-shirt resting on the edge of the bed. Melanie pulled it over her head. The shirt smelled like Chase—ocean and breeze.

She went to find him.

"I need to do laundry," Chase said. He held two steaming cups of hot chocolate in his hands.

Melanie ran her hands down his shirt. "It's fine. I like it."

Chase ambled into his living area and placed the mugs on the coffee table. His couches were black leather. She liked the contrast against the white tiles.

"Tell me about Uncle."

"Must you be a cop all the time?" she asked, rubbing her bruised hand.

His face softened. "I care about you. You can trust me." Chase held out a hand. Melanie slipped her hand into his and sat next to him.

Chase jumped up and left the room. When he returned, he had gauze and peroxide. Gently, he sanitized her wound and wrapped her injured hand. "There, that should help."

Melanie felt good being taken care of. "Thanks." She sipped her hot cocoa and debated how to answer Chase's question about Uncle. She drank half before putting it down. Without looking his way, she began to tell her story matter-of-factly. Only her parents knew her story.

"I was born normal. I could hear like everyone else." She wrinkled her nose at the word, *normal*. Nevertheless, she continued, "When I was five years old, I lived with my birth mother, Janet King. I shared her bed until she met Uncle. Whenever Uncle came over, I had to sleep in a closet."

Melanie choked back tears. Her recent ordeal was too fresh on her mind. She felt Chase's hand on her back and felt comforted.

"I didn't like the closet. It was funky and dark. But Mama made me sleep in there. One night I had to pee. I had to go so bad and I couldn't hold it. I snuck out of the closet and tried to wake Mama. But she was … high … and drunk. She couldn't hear me. Uncle woke up and yelled at me. His voice boomed and I was so frightened, I went all over myself."

Chase tapped her. She looked at him. "Uncle was furious. Said I was too smart to be so nasty. So he punched me on my ear. He punched me on both ears for not listening."

Chase's eyes widened.

She sipped her tepid cocoa and she trudged on. "I screamed so hard Mama awakened. She tried to fight Uncle off but he pushed her against the wall and she passed out. Then he punched me. He punched and punched … and punched." Her voice broke. "He punched my ears until I passed out."

Melanie had no idea how she had tears left to cry after her time in the closet. Chase enfolded her in his arms. "He kept … punching … until I … I passed out." She hiccupped the words. "I passed out and I never heard again."

Chase made sure she could see him. The agony in his face made fresh tears fall. "That's horrible. I can't imagine the sick monster that would harm an innocent child. How could Rachel know all this and lock you in a closet?" he asked.

"She doesn't know. I've only told my parents, and now you." Melanie touched his cheek. "I woke up in the hospital screaming. I remember the panic when I realized I couldn't hear. I begged and begged Dr. James to fix me."

She shuddered. "Oh, God. This is hard." But the words continue to pour from her. "I met the Benson's when I was in the hospital. They had adopted another daughter, Tricia, who was also deaf. They adopted me and introduced me to God. Lainey King was now Melanie Benson. Transformed and renewed. I went through therapy and all that but I found peace when I accepted Christ in my life."

"Please tell me they arrested the creep who did that to you?"

Melanie was taken aback by the venom in Chase's eyes. She patted his arm and felt him relax.

"No. Uncle was ... untouchable. I never saw him after that day but for years his face plagued my nightmares. Uncle is out there somewhere but my mother is still in jail. She served her time for neglecting me but she can't seem to keep out of jail."

"Do you hear from her?"

"She sends me letters, but I leave them unopened."

His eyebrows furrowed. "Why don't you read them?"

"What can my mother say to me that will make everything okay?"

Chase shook his head. "I don't know. Maybe she's sorry."

Melanie gave a sad smile. "Sorry won't give me my hearing back."

11

"You're doing what?" Chase bellowed. He knew Melanie could not hear his yell but she could read the rage on his face. "Rachel kidnapped a helpless child and locked you in a closet. She's guilty and that's why the judge denied her bail. You screamed most of the night and now you want to help her?"

They stood in his kitchen, Chase by the counter and Melanie sat on one of the stools in the center island. "She's my sister. I spoke with Tricia this morning and she agrees with me."

"Rachel's a traitor and home wrecker. I can't believe you're helping her pay for an attorney. You should be filing charges against her as well for false imprisonment." Chase ran his hand across the stubble lining his cheeks. Lord, help him. Why hadn't he remembered relationships were infuriating?

"She made a mistake," Melanie defended.

Chase stormed over to her. "You can forgive Rachel but not your mother?"

"Yes. Rachel loves me. My mother didn't give two cents about me. Janet loved drugs and heroin. Not me. Rachel is family."

"Rachel committed a felony. She could face lifetime

imprisonment."

Melanie jutted her chin and looked away.

His nostrils flared as his temper kicked in. Oh, no. Melanie was not going to end the argument. She was going to look at him. Chase cupped her chin and made her face him. His chest heaved as he looked into her hazel eyes.

"I don't have much family. I have a small circle of people who love me and Rachel is one of them. I just met you. You don't have a say."

She was right. He did not have a say. But he wanted to.

Chase thought of his father and backed down. Ted had made his share of mistakes and Chase stuck by him. Ted was his blood. "I wish I could say I don't understand but I can relate. You say you have a small circle, but mine is limited to one and God." Chase was willing to widen his sphere to one more. "You have me," he said, "if you want me."

Her eyes warmed. "And, you have me."

"I know we've had serious drama but we survived the longest day ever. I'm going to put in for some personal days and decompress. I'd like to take you out on a real date."

Melanie nodded. "I'd like that." She looked at the clock. "How about we get breakfast?"

"Or, I could whip us up some omelets."

"You cook?"

"Yes, my mother made sure to teach me and my

brother, Vincent. She said we both needed to know our way around a kitchen."

"You have a brother?" Melanie asked.

Chase realized she was prodding for information. He hunched his shoulders. "Yes, Vincent. He was two years older than I am. He and my mother were killed in an automobile accident." He lowered his head before remembering Melanie needed to see him. "My father was driving."

Her eyes widened and she cupped her mouth. "I'm sorry." Melanie slid off her stool and walked up to him. Then she opened her arms. Chase stepped into them accepting her warmth and comfort before ending the embrace. He had a jolt he had not experienced in his thirty-one years. Melanie felt like home. That was an adjustment in his thinking. Chase looked into her earnest brown eyes. One he did not mind making.

"How did your dad cope with being responsible for their deaths?"

"He was a mess. Guilt rode him for years." Chase's chest tightened. He never spoke about this with anyone but Melanie had opened up to him. He could do the same.

"Melanie, my father was driving drunk. The three of them had been here, celebrating me buying my home. As usual, my father drank too much but he swore he was able to drive. Both Vincent and my mother insisted he give up the keys. But, my father is stubborn. He's one of those alpha males. 'I'm used to driving when I've had a few,' he'd said." Chase shook his head. "My mother gave in because it was easier than arguing with him. Vincent jumped into the backseat at the last minute. My parents live about ten minutes from here. Ten minutes …"

The familiar pain squeezed his stomach. Chase released a freeing breath. *I am delivered and I'm walking in my deliverance.*

"For almost two years, I froze my father out of my life. I wanted nothing more to do with him. My father was what you would call a controlled drunk. At work, he was a decorated cop. He was the best. But once he came home …" Chase gulped. He needed a minute. The memories were hitting him hard.

Chase walked to the refrigerator to get some orange juice. Seeing the container of eggs, he decided to boil them instead of making omelets. Chase held up the eggs for Melanie to see.

She put two fingers in the air. Chase nodded and placed four eggs in a pot to boil. He reached for two glasses and poured them orange juice, then checked the breadbox. He had a loaf of honey wheat bread. Good. He would make toast when the eggs were ready.

Chase finished his tale. It felt good talking about it to someone. "Three years ago, my dad called me to tell me he had accepted Christ. He told me he was a changed man." He chuckled. "Of course, I didn't believe him. I didn't think he could ever change. What? Give up alcohol? Not Ted Lawson.

"But he had. I gave him two weeks max and he would be back in the bottle. Well, Dad proved me wrong. A month went by and he was sober. Then two. Before I knew it, a year had passed. On his one-year anniversary, I gave my life to the Lord. I realized it was time for me to get my act together. I didn't drink but I was … I …" How could he say this? Chase squinted his eyes. He would go with the truth. "I was a womanizer—a man-whore."

Melanie's eyes widened. "How many women were there?"

Chase shook his head. "It's in the past. I'm disease free and now there is only you. I haven't been seeing anyone in the two years since I've accepted Christ."

Her mouth formed an O. "Two years? That's a long time without …"

Chase crooked his head. "What about you?"

Melanie held up three fingers. "I've had three long-term relationships. My last serious relationship was while I was in college. But … we called it quits. No real reason. We drifted apart."

He narrowed his eyes. Her body language said something different. She twirled her hair around her fingers and shifted her gaze.

He tapped the island counter to get her attention. "You broke up when your father had his heart attack, didn't you?"

Melanie bit her lip. Then she nodded. "Roger wanted to plan a wedding and move to New York. I told him my father needed surgery. Roger refused to understand so … we parted ways."

How much had she given up? Rachel's words came back to him. "You gave up your fiancée and your dreams?" He shook his head. What father would allow her to do that?

"It was my choice." Melanie pointed to her chest.

"I have no regrets."

Chase pushed. "But, I've seen you dance—"

"Are the eggs ready?" she asked.

Chase knew the conversation was closed for now. He nodded and went to look about their breakfast. He would drop the matter but he filed this topic away for future discussion. Melanie needed to dance like she needed to breathe.

***

She could feel Chase's eyes on her back as she went into the bank to fill out leave forms. Chase had already called off to recuperate. She was taking the rest of the week off. Nancy rolled her eyes but Melanie never asked for time. Rachel's face was all over the news. Nancy knew Melanie would be by her friend's side.

Melanie checked on Rachel's funds in case the judge approved bail. Rachel entrusted Melanie with her accounts. Melanie had invested some of Rachel's money and had made Rachel a decent sum. However, Melanie knew defense attorneys were costly. She also withdrew some of her money.

Next Chase drove her to pick up her vehicle from Rachel's place. He had not been able to reach Judd. They stood by Melanie's Infiniti.

"Rachel doesn't need your help," he said. "She needs God and a lawyer."

"Rachel's been in my life for thirteen years. I'm not

turning my back on her." Melanie folded her arms.

Chase backed off. "You're right. As you've pointed out, I have no say."

"I'm going home to shower and change."

"I'll come with you."

She felt suffocated. "Listen, I'm not used to this. I do my own thing. I don't need a shadow."

His face softened. "I know I'm coming on strong but after your ordeal, I don't think you should be alone. I promise to be on my best behavior and support you. Let me tag along."

She read the sincerity in Chase's eyes but she needed her space. "My sister, Tricia, will come with me." Chase gave a curt nod. She knew she was freezing him out but Chase was … intense. Melanie was attracted but things were moving too fast.

"I'll call you," she said.

Chase looked like he wanted to say more but instead he gave her a hug. "I'll be praying for you." She saw his head move toward her lips and turned her head. Chase caught the slight. His face twisted like he was hurt before he forced out a smile. He gave a small wave and left.

Why was she pushing him away? Last night she had opened up to Chase and told him her secret pain. Melanie wondered about that while driving home. Chase cared about her. She could see it in his eyes. She cared for him as well. She cared so much for him it shook her bones. Maybe that's why she was so scared.

Chase had the power to hurt her and Melanie could

not let that happen. Janet had hurt her. Rachel had hurt her. She could not—would not—give Chase that same power.

12

"Thanks for coming to get me." Judd folded his long body into Chase's Jeep. "I didn't want Nadine driving me home."

Chase narrowed his eyes. "You stayed there all night?" He asked the obvious question.

Judd jerked his head. "Yeah. I ... I didn't want her to be alone. Her parents are staying at the Westin."

Chase could not see Peter and Marie leaving their only daughter alone. Unless ... "You slept with her," Chase accused.

Judd looked out the window. "When Nadine came over to me, she whispered to me that she wanted me to stay. She said I made her feel safe. I couldn't say no."

"You took advantage of a woman in distress." Chase jabbed him on the arm. "How could you?" A raindrop splattered across the windshield. A second later there was a downpour. Used to the erratic Florida weather, Chase turned on the wipers. He needed Rain-X.

"Believe me when I say I didn't. If anything, Nadine took advantage of me. She said she needed me. *She* seduced *me.*"

"Uhm hmm." Chase found that hard to believe. He

pressed the defrost button and adjusted the temperature.

"Where's your woman?" Judd asked.

Judd mentioning Melanie was the perfect distraction.

"Melanie's off with her sister to help Rachel," Chase said.

"Wow," was Judd's eloquent response.

Chase released his fury. "Rachel lied to her and kidnaps a child. Then she locks Melanie in a closet for hours and Melanie still wants to help her."

"You don't know a thing about girlfriends, do you?" Judd laughed. "Women stick together. They fuss, fight, and tell each other off but in the next instant they're hugging and crying and all that."

"Rachel broke the law." The rain eased. Chase decreased the wiper speed.

"Women are a law unto themselves." Judd looked his way. "Don't tell me you tried to stop her."

Chase gripped the wheel.

"Oh snap. You're lucky you still have your head." Judd laughed. "If it's one thing I know, you don't come between a woman and her friend. And if a woman has her mind made up about something, you don't try to change her mind."

Judd's laughter was getting on his nerves. "Now you tell me," Chase muttered. "How do you know so much about women anyway?"

"Did you not meet my mother and four sisters?

Four. I learned to smile, nod, and shut up."

Chase pictured Judd's large family. He had met them all when he went with Judd to Louisiana for a family reunion. Judd was right. Chase had not gotten a word in with all those independent women. Chase grinned. "I don't think I said one complete sentence while I was around them."

"Yeah, Momma, Diana, Winnie, Tasha, and Aubrey are a trip," Judd said. "You know Winnie was sweet on you."

Chase eyes widened. "No. You could've told me. All your sisters are fine."

Judd grinned. "Now you know why I'm a mean fight." Chase pulled up in front of Judd's trailer park. The white trailer looked small on the outside, but the inside was large and spacious and suited Judd just fine.

"You coming in?" Judd asked.

"No. I'm going to see my dad."

Judd nodded. He opened the door and put one leg out. Then he looked back at Chase. "Don't worry about Melanie. She'll be all right."

Chase cleared his throat. "I worry about her. I know I just met her but I want to protect her. I can't explain it."

Judd smiled. "It's finally happening, my friend. You're falling in love."

If this is love, he could do without it. His insides were twisted and he felt like a goldfish in a bowl—swimming in circles and not getting anywhere. "Why didn't you warn me that love was torturous and a pain?"

"Love is the most beautiful, horrible thing."

Chase shook his head. "I don't know if I'm in love though. It's way too soon."

Judd had a faraway look on his face. "How long does it take to fall in love? Sometimes love comes like a bowling ball and hit you flat on your a— butt."

They shared an awkward laugh. "Get out of my Jeep. You're getting too mushy for me." Chase pushed Judd out of the vehicle. Judd landed in the wet mud.

Judd flipped to his feet. "See how fast you got me on my butt. I love you, man."

Chase's strength was no match for Judd's. He was rock solid, so Chase knew Judd was playing along.

"Love you, too." Chase put on his shades as the sun forced its way through the clouds. He knew his face was crimson red. "I've got to get out of here." He pinned Judd with a steel gaze. "Stay away from Nadine."

Judd's cell phone beeped at the same time.

"Speaking of..." Judd winked. "It's not me who needs the warning. Catch you later."

Chase watched Judd's confident stride. He sure hoped Judd knew what he was doing. Nadine's parents looked like their lineage went back to the founding fathers. Chase did not know how they would feel about Nadine dating Judd, the cop from the trailer park. He said a quick prayer for his friend before driving to his father's house. He parked beside Ted's 2007 black F-150.

When Chase strolled into his father's house, he half-expected to see his mother wearing her hair bonnet and wiping her hands on her apron. Violet Lawson would hold his face and kiss his cheeks, inevitably leaving a dash of flour or gravy on his face. Chase and Vincent had grown up here.

Chase smiled. It was so good to have a home. A refuge. He sauntered into the kitchen and traced his hands over the Pillsbury Doughboy cookie jar. He had carved it out of Balsa wood before painting it blue and white. Chase saw imperfections in his handiwork, but Violet loved it. His eyes scanned the Pillsbury Doughboy oven mitts and kitchen towels. Chase peered through the blue and white-checkered curtains, which provided a view to the patio.

His father was out there tending to his mother's vegetable and spice garden. Ted said it made him feel close to Violet. Chase pushed the screen door and stepped outside.

Ted held up a hand in greeting. He wore blue jeans and a flannel shirt. Ted used the back of his hand to wipe the sweat lining his forehead.

Chase reached into the cooler his father kept stocked with ice and water. He grabbed one for himself and for his dad.

"The ants got me," Ted said, coming into the patio.

Chase handed his dad the water then sat on one of the lounge stairs. "They are silent and deadly. That's why I traded in my push lawnmower for the ride. I couldn't take the ants."

"Glad to see you cracked the case," Ted said.

"Almost always the parent. It's such a shame." He took a swig from his water bottle and sat on another vacant chair.

Chase gulped his water down before crushing the plastic. "I was there until the wee hours of the morning but it was worth it. Steven is back at home and safe and the culprits are behind bars."

"I saved you some fish from yesterday," Ted said. "I knew when you didn't come by you were making headway into the case."

Chase smiled. "You taught me well."

"How's the hulk?" Ted asked.

"I think Judd's in love." Chase laughed.

Ted's eyes widened. "I never thought he would get bitten."

Chase cracked up. Love definitely had a bite. He sobered. "Dad, I've met someone."

Ted turned to face him. "Really? What's she like?"

"Everything and then some," Chase replied. He knew he had a goofy expression on his face. "Melanie is beautiful, brave, and feisty. She's also deaf."

Chase studied his father's face to gauge his reaction.

"Deaf?" Ted rubbed his chin. "There's no perfect woman. Just perfect for you. How do you communicate?"

Chase relaxed. He did not realize how tense he was about his father's opinion. "Melanie reads lips. She wasn't born deaf. Some jerk beat her badly when she was young. She speaks and texts. We use FaceTime for

110

phone calls. I plan on learning sign language though."

"You have some wicked people out there. Thank God for deliverance. I feel anybody who hurts a child should be hanged," Ted said. "But, I'm happy to hear you've found someone. It's not good for you to be alone. If it's meant to be, it will work. Time has a way of telling all things."

Ted was right. If only Chase were more patient.

"Does she have all her teeth?" Ted asked.

Chase chuckled. He tossed the plastic container toward his father in jest. "Melanie has a smile that lights up her face. And, she's an amazing dancer. She flies through the air. I can't explain it … put it into words." He touched his chest. "I just know it here."

"That's how I felt about Violet." Ted smiled. "The moment I laid eyes on Violet Wallen I knew she was the one."

Chase heard the tenderness in his father's tone. He changed the conversation. "If you knew that Mom was the one, why did you cheat on her?"

Ted clasped his hands. "Men are idiots. Honestly, alcohol dictated a huge part of my life. Your mother never touched a bottle and she hated to see me drink. So, like other addicts, I found somewhere to go. I usually ended up in someone else's arms. A good part of my youth was spent in a stupor. I don't know how I survived."

"You survived because of Mom and God. God meant for you to survive." Chase knew Violet Lawson held the home together with prayers and a firm hand. She never bad-mouthed Ted. Instead, Violet made Ted a hero until Chase and Vincent discovered the truth at ten and twelve. Even then Violet demanded they honor their father. But growing up with an alcoholic made Chase stay away from the bottle.

"Your mother was my angel. She prayed so much she kept me up at night." Ted smiled.

"That sounds like Mom," Chase said.

Ted crumbled. "And now I have to look myself in the mirror every morning knowing I killed two people I loved most in the world. It's torture. If I weren't a cop ..." Ted gulped. "I knew what to say and do to get out of jail time. I *lied* to avoid jail. I'm a selfish bas— creep."

Chase held out his hands. "Dad, quit beating up yourself. God has thrown all that mess in the sea of forgetfulness and you need to do the same."

"God has forgotten, but I remember. Sometimes I wonder, when am I going to pay? I was a horrible father and husband. Not all the time, but ..."

"Dad, I know I sound selfish but I'm glad you're not in jail," Chase said. "And even if you were, I would still stand by you because you're family."

Suddenly, Melanie's reasoning made sense. Chase understood why she was standing by Rachel.

Ted gave a sad smile. "Thanks, son. Your devotion means the world to me. But I know your mother's death still affects you. You haven't made anything since Violet's death. Don't think I haven't noticed that."

"I will one day," Chase whispered. Ted told the truth. Chase had not touched a piece of wood since he had buried his mother and brother. He went and hugged his father. "Please stop torturing yourself. Mom wouldn't have wanted this. Remember the good times. You'll see Mom in heaven."

"I know, but I wish Violet were here to see me going to church. Your mother invited me so many times but the bottle was more appealing." He looked Chase in the eyes. "Son, be wise in your actions. The last thing I want you to have is regret. Regret is a hard cookie to eat. It'll crack your teeth for sure."

"Speaking of eating," Chase said, attempting to lighten the air, "let me get a taste of that fish." He patted his stomach. "I had a light breakfast."

Ted gestured for Chase to follow him inside. He took the red snapper out the refrigerator, then fetched bread, tomato, and onions. Chase retrieved two plates, glasses, and utensils from the cupboard. They set up on the kitchen table.

"Get the *Great Value* cranberry black cherry juice," Ted commanded. "I don't know what Wal-Mart put in that drink but I must drink a couple glasses every day."

"I agree. You have me hooked on it, too." Chase laughed. "Judd calls it crack juice."

Ted shook his head. "Judd is a piece of work."

Chase and Ted washed their hands and blessed the food. The snapper was fresh and delicious.

"So, when am I going to meet Melanie?" Ted asked, biting into his fish sandwich.

"Soon. I hope," Chase said. "I planned to take her on our first date sometime this week but I think I might have scared her off. I might be coming on too strong."

Ted nodded. "Yup. Sounds just like you. When you were young if you wanted something, you zoned in on it until it was yours. I call it intensity."

"Melanie will call it obsession if I don't give her breathing room," Chase joked. His joke was half-serious. Melanie said she would call but Chase wondered if that was code for, *I'm running as far away from you as I can.*

Ted leaned forward. "Chase, I'm going to give you the best advice of your life. Give Melanie her space. It sounds like you're falling in love for the first time and you're eager. But, listen to the voice of experience."

Chase jutted his jaw. "I've never felt this way before. I can't afford for someone to snatch her up."

Ted shook his head. "A woman is delicate like a butterfly." He lowered his voice. "Have you ever seen a *really* beautiful butterfly?"

Chase nodded though he was unsure where his father was going with the butterfly analogy.

Ted continued, "A butterfly is so beautiful that you want to catch it, hold onto it tight. But if you do, you'll crush it and it'll die. The key is to keep your hand open." Ted opened his palm. "The butterfly will flitter around here, there, and this way and that. But if you're patient, eventually the butterfly will land right into your hand."

13

Tricia's eyes bulged. She signed, "Wow. Look at that brother dressed in green. He looks like he's made of all muscles."

Melanie and Tricia stood outside the jailhouse in Punta Gorda. Rachel had been transported there after her booking to await arraignment. It was 9:37 a.m. and the sun was on full blast. Melanie wore a pink chiffon dress with gold flats. She eyed Tricia's white leggings.

Melanie poked Tricia's arm then pointed to Tricia's still-flat stomach. "You're married and pregnant."

"That doesn't mean my eyes have stopped working," Tricia signed.

Melanie stifled her giggles. The officer was fine. And *huge*. He walked towards them and smiled, showing a set of Colgate-commercial-ready teeth.

"I can't believe Rachel won't see us," Melanie said. "This is our second day here and she refuses."

"She thinks we're going to chew her out. I told you to call Chase."

Officer Dark Chocolate froze. He turned to them. "Did you mean Chase Lawson?"

Tricia nodded. He stood outside Melanie's vision,

so Tricia interpreted for Melanie.

"Chase is my partner. Can I help you?"

"Tell him," Tricia signed.

Melanie folded her arms. The officer came in her direct line of vision. "Are you Melanie, by chance?" he asked.

Melanie eyes widened. She gave a quick nod. "This is my sister, Tricia," she said.

"I'm Judd," he said. "Chase did not exaggerate. You're beautiful." He swung his gaze between both of them. "You both are."

Tricia preened under Judd's compliment. Melanie felt pleased that Chase had spoken about her but she was too obstinate to show it.

"Our friend Rachel was arrested," Tricia signed and spoke. "We came to visit her but she won't see us."

"Ah. I see," Judd said. He crooked his head. "Come with me."

Tricia smiled triumphantly and pinched Melanie's arm. Like soldiers, they marched behind Judd inside the jailhouse.

"Judd said we should wait here," Tricia said.

Melanie watched Judd chat with the officer on duty. Within minutes, they were being ushered into a private room. Rachel was transported in to meet them. When Melanie saw Rachel, her mouth dropped open. Rachel was dressed in gray prison garb and her lip was busted. The officer undid her cuffs.

"Only because you're Chase's girlfriend," the officer

said. "This isn't normally done."

Judd stepped inside. "I'll be here. My case isn't up for another hour." He took a seat in the furthest corner of the room and pulled out his cell phone.

"You have thirty minutes," the officer said. Then he left and shut the door.

"Rachel." Melanie rushed to hug her friend.

Rachel stiffened, but Melanie was not going to let her go. Tricia rushed over and the three women hugged. They broke down. Rachel's body heaved against her. Tears threatened to spill but Melanie remained strong for Rachel.

Tricia's face was red and puffy. "Look at us. We're a mess," she signed.

Rachel took a deep breath and ran her hands through her limp hair. "I miss you guys."

"What happened to your lip?" Tricia reached out to touch the scar.

"Some of the women do not appreciate me kidnapping someone's child," Rachel explained. She shrugged. "I'm all right."

"Why'd you refuse to see us?" Melanie asked.

Rachel lowered her eyes. "I couldn't look the both of you in the eyes especially after what I've done," she signed and glanced at Melanie. "How can you be here after I locked you in a closet?"

In one breath, Melanie said, "It's okay," then, in another, said, "Rachel I can't believe you locked me in a closet. How could you? I was stuck in that tight space

Michelle Lindo-Rice

for hours. *Hours*. I bruised my hand banging on the door." Melanie clutched her chest. "If Chase hadn't called my phone, you would've left me there. How could you? We've been friends for years and you sold me out over money?"

Rachel lowered her eyes before she signed, "I'm sorry, Melanie.

Tears filled Melanie's eyes. "I'm claustrophobic. I felt like I was going to pass out."

"I wasn't thinking. I ... I panicked," Rachel said.

Melanie trembled. "Even if you panicked and locked me in there, when you got caught, why didn't you tell someone where I was? I could've died."

"That was a wicked thing to do, Rachel," Tricia said. "Wicked and cruel. If it were me, I wouldn't be trying to help you." She frowned at Melanie. "Why didn't you tell me what she did to you? I would've stayed my butt home."

"I get it, Tricia," Rachel said. "I'm in jail with a busted lip. Don't you think I'm suffering enough?"

Tricia jutted her chin. "No."

Melanie shoved her terror to the back of her mind. Rachel had no way of knowing about her past experience in a closet. "Rachel, I love you. You're my sister. Nothing will change that. I'm mad at you but I still had to come."

Tricia rolled her eyes. Melanie could feel the heat emanating off her body. "Why would you help Francis kidnap a child? Your face is plastered all over the news. From the sound of things, they're putting everything on

118

you."

Rachel's eyes widened. "Francis showed up at my door with Steven. I should've never agreed to his plan. I had no idea he was going to—"

Melanie interrupted. "Stop lying, Rachel. You were all about the ransom money. You had to be in on it. That's why you locked me in the closet."

"No! I admit I got greedy when I heard about the hundred thousand dollars. Francis convinced me I would get away with it," Rachel said. "I was an accomplice *after* the fact. I was trying to help Francis out."

Melanie glared. "You're a grown woman. Own up to your wrongdoings. You could have said no. You are an accomplice. Period. You could've called the cops but not once did you think about Nadine. Steven's mother. Remember her? You were all about helping your married boyfriend. So, unless you have something on Francis, you're going down."

"She didn't know," Tricia signed. "Take it easy."

Melanie narrowed her eyes. "Don't go defending her, now. You were just chewing her out. Before a couple days ago, I thought I knew Rachel, but she's not who we thought she was."

"She's human," Trisha said. "One who fell into temptation and worthy of forgiveness just like anybody else."

"I'm sorry, Melanie," Rachel said. "You're right. I knew better than to sleep with Francis. God spoke to me through scriptures and messages but I ignored all His warnings." Her shoulders slumped. "Now my career is ruined. I called my mother in Texas. That was the most shameful phone call of my life. Mom told me I deserved whatever happens to me. Her new husband's rich and she's not asking him to help me with money or the attorney fees. Besides you two, I have no one in my corner."

Melanie thawed. "I'm furious but I'm here. I accessed your funds from all your accounts. Then I pulled some of mine." She patted Rachel's hand. "You should be all right, for now."

Fresh tears brimmed in Rachel's eyes. "Thank you, Melanie. I can't believe you're helping me after what I did. I'll give you Skip's contact information."

"Don't thank me. Thank God," Melanie said. "He spoke to my heart. God reminded me of all the wonderful things I love about you. The good outweighs the bad. As for Skip, I'm sure I'll be able to get his contact info off Google."

"What does Skip say you should do?" Tricia asked.

"Skip advised me to plead guilty and rat out Francis." Rachel twisted her hands.

"Skip is right," Melanie said. "It's time for you to squeal. Whatever it takes to help your case."

"I—I love him." Rachel's lips quivered. "It pains me to turn against Francis."

Melanie ranted. "Francis only cares about himself. The quicker you realize that—"

Tricia tapped Melanie on the shoulder and shook her head. Melanie rolled her eyes but stopped her tirade.

"Telling the truth is the only thing that will help you now, Rachel," Tricia said. "The truth shall set you free."

"Or in this case, keep me locked up behind bars," Rachel signed. Melanie knew Rachel spoke the truth.

Rachel looked Tricia's way. "Enough about me. Tell me how Baby is doing."

Recognizing Rachel needed the distraction, Melanie and Tricia changed the conversation and detailed Tricia's pregnancy woes. However, it was never far from Melanie's mind that Rachel could spend years behind bars.

Lord, please make a way, somehow.

14

HEY, YOUR GIRL IS AT THE JAILHOUSE.

Chase read Judd's text.

MELANIE? He texted back.

DO YOU HAVE ANOTHER GIRLFRIEND I DON'T KNOW ABOUT?

Judd was such a smart mouth.

Chase had spent the day puttering about his house. He had repaired a leaky faucet, dusted all the ceiling fans, and fixed the screen door to his lanai. He had read his Bible and prayed for an hour that morning. Chase was doing as his father said—giving Melanie her space. But he had to keep busy or go crazy. His fingers itched to pick up his wood carving kit, but Chase deflected.

He had been about to mow his lawn when Judd's text came in. He penned a quick reply.

AT THIS POINT I'M NOT SURE I CAN CALL HER THAT. Chase cringed. His words sounded pitiful but he had to talk to someone about Melanie. Thinking about her was his newest pastime. Chase needed to voice those thoughts aloud.

CALLING YOU IN FIVE.

OK.

Chase strolled into the kitchen, rested his cell phone on the counter, and washed his hands. Then he opened his refrigerator to get a bottled water. Chase wandered over to the counter and picked up his phone.

He looked at the screen willing Judd to call.

Soon Judd's face flashed on his screen. Chase swiped the answer button. "Took you long enough."

"I was inside the room with Melanie, Rachel, and Tricia."

"That's Melanie's sister," Chase supplied.

"I got them in to see Rachel as a favor," Judd said. "What're you up to? I'm off the clock and could use a bite to eat. Hint, hint."

Chase opened his freezer. "I've got some steaks I can throw on the grill. Grab a bag of salad and some ginger ale."

"Salad. Ginger ale. Got it. See you in a bit." Judd disconnected the line.

Chase threw the steaks in a bowl of cold water and poured in white vinegar. His mother used vinegar to clean poultry, fish, and just about everything else. While the meat thawed, Chase chopped up onions and garlic. He gathered his spices and olive oil. Chase mixed his ingredients together. He reached for the bowl, poured the water out, and seasoned the steaks. He would grill them frozen.

Chase had just fired up the charcoal grill in his backyard when Judd came through his lanai. The screen door closed behind him. Judd had a spare key so he had let himself inside.

Judd peered at Chase and said, "You look like a lost puppy dog. You make falling in love real undesirable."

"Shut up. You don't look too good yourself." Chase observed Judd's tired, red eyes. "Have you slept the last couple days?"

Judd shook his head and went to sit in a chair around the glass table on the lawn. It was the kind that came with the huge umbrella in the middle. "I've been sneaking off to see Nadine when Steven's asleep."

"You know that's wrong on so many different levels," Chase said. "The first time you slept with her, I'll say it was a mistake. A result of an emotional night. But twice? Did you forget you arrested her husband?"

Judd yawned. "I know. I was there. You don't have to remind me of the details."

"Doesn't it bother you?" Chase asked.

"Of course it does. But, then Nadine looks up at me with those sad eyes of hers. I—I like her."

"You *like* her. For how long?" Judd was a serial dater. Since Chase had known Judd Armstrong, he had never had a serious relationship.

Chase checked the temperature of the charcoal. They looked ashy. Perfect. Carefully, Chase placed the frozen meat on the grill, then closed it. He would turn them every few minutes.

Dusting his hands on his jeans, Chase joined Judd at the table. "Aren't you going to answer me?"

"I don't know." Judd would not meet Chase's gaze. "This is different. I feel *things.*"

"Things," Chase teased.

"Kind of what you're feeling." Judd coughed.

Chase laughed. "You can't say the words. Can you?"

"Can you?" Judd redirected the question at Chase.

Chase touched his chin. "I wouldn't call it love but it's a strong like. I can't stop thinking about Melanie. I'm into her. It's like I want to see her every day. I want to talk about her all the time."

"If it sounds like a duck ..." Judd trailed off.

Chase felt it was time for a conversation change. "Well this discussion might be pointless. Like I told you, she needs her space."

Judd's eyes bulged. "When I saw her earlier—and she's fine as ever, by the way—Melanie looked as if she were in good spirits. I mean she told Rachel off but within five minutes, all three women were hugging and talking about Tricia's baby." Judd chuckled. "I'll never understand the female psyche."

Chase did not like hearing about Melanie's sunny mood while he was in misery. He missed her. Was this all one-sided? "Let me check on the steaks," he said. He needed a moment from Judd's prying eyes.

The steaks were seared well on one side. He went into the house to get the Sonny's BBQ sauce out of the refrigerator and grabbed a bowl, platter, and basting brush.

The screen door creaked behind him on his way out. Judd was by the grill. "I make my own sauce that would make you eat your fingers."

"You're always bragging about how you can cook. I've yet to see you make anything."

"I cooked for Nadine."

Chase's eyes widened. "I've known you for seven years and you've never cooked. Nadine hasn't known you for seven days and she gets the royal treatment."

"That's because you can't give me what she can." Judd waggled his eyebrows.

Chase basted the steaks with the sauce. They were almost ready. "Shameful."

Judd punched him on the arm. "Don't be jealous because you're not getting any. No one told you to get all sanctified and holy."

Chase narrowed his eyes. "I don't regret it. Not for a minute. I'm a better man because of God. You should try Him sometimes. As a matter of fact, I'm going to up my prayers on your behalf."

Judd shrugged. "Have at it."

Chase rested the steaks on the Martha Stewart platter. His mom had purchased it on sale at Macy's for him. Chase smiled thinking of Violet. He closed the grill and then closed the shutters so the flames would cool. Judd collected the bowl and sauce. The men went inside.

Judd retrieved the salad and soda from the refrigerator. Chase made up their plates and blessed the food. The men dug into their meal.

Chase thought of Francis and Rachel. "When are Francis and Rachel being arraigned?"

"On the 29th. Francis's time is at nine o'clock and Rachel's scheduled for ten. They're both going before Judge Wilkinson. I'll be there. Nadine is going as well."

Judge Wilkinson would not be lenient. Chase knew that from being involved in cases in his courtroom before.

"I should go. I can't miss that," Chase said. Plus, he wanted to see Melanie. He knew she would be there to support.

Chase's concern must have showed on his face.

"You care for her," Judd said.

Chase nodded. "Every news station in Southwest Florida will be there. There'll be added police presence at the courthouse, which means there'll be chaos. Rachel and Francis' story is way past sensational. I have to be there in case Melanie needs me."

Judd pointed to his steak. "This is good." Then he continued, "Melanie will need you. I was there today. Those women are tighter than a dancer's rear end. Melanie is going to breakdown and she'll be glad to see your face."

"A dancer's rear end?" Chase laughed. "Only you would use an analogy like that."

"I got my point across, didn't I?"

Chase nodded. With a distinct lack of confidence, Chase said, "I hope Melanie doesn't see my being there as pushy."

Judd shook his head. "We're the arresting officers. We're expected to be there. Now finish that steak so we can catch a game on TV or something. We need to pump up the testosterone level because you sound whipped."

Chase would argue but Judd was right. He was whipped and every part of him ached. The dilemma was the one who caused the ache was the only one with the cure.

15

"Baby's hungry," Tricia said, patting her stomach.

When Melanie and Tricia left the courthouse, they headed straight to Skip's Punta Gorda office and settled the fees. The women had just departed Skip's office when Tricia's stomach growled.

Melanie rolled her eyes. "Stop putting everything on the baby. You know you used to eat like a farmer before you were pregnant. Lucky for you, you're as thin as a reed."

Tricia laughed. "Stop being a hater and feed us."

Melanie merged onto traffic on US 41. Ten minutes later she crossed the bridge into Port Charlotte.

Melanie turned into The Soup Jungle Café. It was a mom and pop joint near the huge Bingo building. Soup Jungle served everything from salads and pizzas to subs and wraps. Melanie swerved as she parked in one of the spots, which said, *No Bingo Parking*. Arm-in-arm, they entered the restaurant.

The smell of grease hit Melanie's nose. The café smelled of French fries and grilled chicken. Her mouth watered. The place could use a paint job and the monkeys, lions, and tigers hanging from the ceiling could be replaced. But who cared when the food was so good?

Melanie waved at the owner/waitress, Minka, and scanned the chalkboard. The soup of the day was Italian. She always read the sign even though she always ordered one of two things—the Mediterranean salad or the Buffalo wings with fries.

Tricia snagged them a booth in the back. From experience, Minka brought two glasses of Diet Pepsi. "What can I get you ladies?" she asked.

"I should get the salad, but…" Tricia inhaled. "My baby is saying, fries, fries, fries."

Melanie laughed. "I know what you mean."

"Baby wins," Tricia said.

"I'll have a cheeseburger, well-done, with fries. Plus, please add an order of eggplant fries."

Minka wrote down her order and gave Melanie a quick nod.

"I'll have the Mediterranean, with no onions, and the dressing on the side," Melanie said.

"Small or large?" Minka asked.

"I'll take a large salad today," Melanie answered.

Minka went to fulfill their orders.

Tricia signed, "So tell me, when did Chase move to boyfriend status?"

Melanie shook her head. "Chase isn't my boyfriend. One kiss doesn't make—"

Tricia's eyes rounded. "You kissed? When? You didn't tell me about that."

"It was on Monday."

"And today is Thursday and you're just now getting around to telling me?" Tricia's hands flew with her words.

"Uhm, our friend was *arrested*. I think that's more important," Melanie said.

Tricia raised an eyebrow. "Not in my book. It's equally important. Now tell me all about that kiss."

Melanie signed, "It was… toe-curling." She lowered her head. She knew her face had to be red. "Chase knows what he's doing."

Tricia leaned forward. "Wow. That must have been some kiss. When will you see him again?" she signed.

"I told him I needed space." Melanie did not add she had been sleepless in Port Charlotte for nights. She definitely would not mention how she replayed Chase's kiss several times in her mind.

"Space to do what?" Tricia quizzed.

"I'm not trying to have some man I met about a week ago rule my life." Melanie's neck snapped left to right. "Chase felt I shouldn't have helped Rachel. Where does he get off telling me what to do about my friend?"

"I understand why he said that," Tricia said.

Melanie narrowed her eyes.

"Chase is objective. He's looking at Rachel from a different viewpoint. She kidnapped a child and had an affair with a married man. Frankly, Rachel is making Christians look bad."

Their food arrived. Melanie and Tricia thanked the waitress and blessed their meal.

Tricia licked her lips. "This smells so good."

Melanie ate a piece of grilled chicken and closed her eyes. "I forgot how good their food is." When Melanie opened her eyes, Tricia's mouth was stuffed.

"Take your time. The food's not going anywhere," Melanie said before addressing Tricia's earlier comment. "What do you mean Rachel is making Christians look bad?"

"The news media was quick to point out Rachel was our church secretary. Pastor Brooks must be humiliated. I know the members of Ransomed Hope are appalled." Tricia bit into a chicken wing.

"I can't believe she kept her relationship a secret for ten months," Melanie said.

"It's not the first time," Tricia said.

Melanie pierced Tricia with a gaze. "What do you mean?"

Tricia wiped Buffalo sauce off her mouth. "When we were seniors in high school, Rachel had an abortion."

Melanie almost choked on her food. "Wha—What? How do you know?" The words, *Rachel had an abortion,* swirled through her mind.

Tricia nodded. "Rachel told me about a month or two after she did it. Rachel conned her mother into giving her money for the clinic. She was scared to tell you."

"Why?" Melanie furrowed her brows.

"If you had known back then, you would've dropped her as a friend. Rachel knew that and that's why she didn't confide in you."

Melanie blinked. "I wouldn't have agreed to that but apparently anything goes with you."

Tricia glared. "I didn't know about it until after. Rachel couldn't take the guilt and she needed to talk to someone. I have my personal beliefs but I'm not going to turn my back on a friend."

"And I would've?"

"I'm not saying that but you were different then. You would've cut her off."

"Well, I don't know what I would've done," Melanie said. "Rachel didn't give me a chance. Look at what she's done now and I'm here."

"Yes, you are. I know Rachel is grateful for that. But the you back then wouldn't be so understanding."

"You don't know that." Melanie gritted her teeth. The women finished their meal in tense silence. Melanie was glad when the bill came. She dropped twenty-five dollars on the table, grabbed her Coach bag, and stormed out of the restaurant. Tricia was right behind her. Melanie clicked the locks and they entered the vehicle.

Tricia tapped Melanie's arm. Melanie faced her.

"I wouldn't have told you if I knew you would be upset with me. I told you because Rachel isn't as innocent as she claims. I wouldn't put it past Rachel to be the mastermind behind everything," Tricia said.

Melanie sagged. "Rachel should've told me about the baby. I'm hurt she felt she couldn't trust me." She laced her fingers through her curls. "I don't know her. Who is this Rachel? She kept a child hostage and stole another woman's husband."

Tricia's eyes softened. "The same one who locked you in a closet."

Melanie's body heaved. Tricia hugged her while she fell apart. Soon, Tricia pulled away and grasped Melanie's cheeks.

"Rachel still needs us. She needs her friends. Skip said her arraignment is on the 29th. Will you be there?"

Melanie bit her lip to keep from blurting out a big "No." Instead, she closed her eyes and prayed. "Lord, I don't know what to do. I need Your guidance. Help me make the right decision."

Love covers a multitude of sins.

Melanie received the thought breathed into her spirit. She opened her eyes and looked into Tricia's warm ones. "I'm going. I love Rachel even if …" Melanie jutted her chin. Love did not need a reason. Love *is*. It was not dependent on anything.

"I love Rachel. I'll be there," Melanie said.

Tricia smiled. "Tres Amigas."

16

"I plead not guilty, Your Honor," Francis stated into the microphone. He stood next to his defense attorney, David Rufalo.

From his seat in the rear of the courthouse, Chase's eyes widened. He nudged Judd on the arm. Cameras flashed and members of the press scribbled furious notes.

Nadine jumped up from her seat in the front row. "Are you serious?" Before anyone could anticipate her next move, Nadine bounded through the small partition. Her black pants suit helped her pounce on Francis' back with ease. She hammered his head with her fists.

"You monster. I hate your lying, cheating guts," Nadine screamed. Her parents rushed out of their seats. But, the press blocked their path.

"Get off me." Francis grabbed Nadine's hair. Nadine bit his arms. Francis's blood curling scream would be viewed on YouTube across the nation. When she tore her teeth away, his puncture wounds were clearly visible.

Judd vaulted out of his seat and raced toward the melee. The bailiffs' sprung into action, prompting

Chase to remain in his position.

"Stop it this instant!" Judge Wilkinson roared. "Mrs. Ashton, leave my courthouse before I have you arrested for assault." He banged his gravel but Nadine latched like a monkey. It took some effort before the guards pried Nadine off Francis' back. Nadine kicked and screamed before Judd scooped her into his arms.

Judd held onto Nadine as she wept into his arms. He led her out of the courthouse, shielding her face from the flashing cameras. That picture was sure to hit front-page news. Once Judd and Nadine had departed, calmness ensued. Nadine's parents made as dignified an exit as they could, shielding their faces from the cameras.

"Mrs. Ashton will be banned from future proceedings," the judge said. "While I understand her emotional turmoil, I cannot tolerate any outbursts in my courtroom."

"Judge, may we take a break?" David asked. "My client needs emergency care."

Chase had to agree. Francis' Canali classic fit grey stripe suit looked ragged and torn. Nadine had one wicked temper when riled. She-Claw. Judd had met his match.

Judge Wilkinson shook his head. "No break." Then glared at the press. "And, no more cameras. I can't have this circus in my courtroom."

"But—"

The judge held up a hand. "But, nothing. I'll grant Mr. Ashton five minutes to comb his hair and tend to his hand. Then we'll resume with the proceedings."

David nodded. Chase was not surprised at Judge Wilkinson's lack of empathy. Francis and David walked past him huddled together. During the break, Melanie and Tricia slipped inside the courtroom.

Chase eyed Melanie's black jacket, cream undershirt tucked neatly into a figure-hugging black floral skirt, and nude stilettos and gulped. Her eyes widened when she spotted him. Her face held a light blush. Melanie lifted a hand and gave a small wave.

Chase returned the wave before his feet led him in her direction. He nodded at Tricia and reached over to kiss Melanie's cheek. Chase knew he should pull away but he lingered. He smelled coconut and almonds. He placed another light kiss on Melanie's cheek. Then he stepped back.

"Good seeing you," he signed.

Melanie raised a brow. "You're learning sign language," she said.

Chase smiled. "I'm very motivated."

"I think it's sweet," Tricia spoke and signed. She looked around. "I heard Francis' wife attacked him."

Chase nodded. He made sure Melanie could see his lips before answering. "Yes, she was like a ninja in black. Nadine won't be allowed back in court."

"We saw her in the hallway with your partner," Melanie said.

Francis returned into the courtroom.

Chase felt his phone vibrate and pulled it out of his pocket. "That's Judd. I'll be back. Save me a seat," he said to Melanie before going through the door.

"Where are you?" Chase asked. "Are you with She-Claw?" He walked over the huge window and looked down into the courtyard.

"What did you call her?" Judd asked. He did not wait for an answer. "I'm in Nadine's town car. Her parents hired a car service. We just dropped them off at their hotel."

Chase dropped his voice to a whisper. "You need to stay away from her."

"I can't. I can't leave her alone."

"Judd, think about what you're doing. Please."

"I don't want to think. I want to feel."

Chase looked around to make sure he did not have any ears. "She's all over the news. Cool the heat a little. It's all about timing."

"I'll talk to you."

The line went dead.

Chase toyed with his phone. Judd had better be careful. Chase discerned hurt at the end of that romance novel. The Goodman's were not about to sit by and let their precious daughter be with Judd. Chase knew their type. There were few men of color in their circles. Judd lacked money or degrees. His chances of acceptance were slim.

But Judd was his own man. And, Nadine was no pushover. Chase shrugged. He had his own romance to write. Chase realized there was no telling love what to do. His heart was at its mercy.

He returned to the packed courtroom. Melanie

scooted over. It was a tight fit but Chase hunkered down next to her. His thigh grazed hers.

Chase reached over and clasped her hand into his. He gave her a light squeeze and she tensed. Chase groaned. From the corner of his eye, he saw her poked lips. Too bad. He was holding on tight. Chase wanted to kiss Melanie's pink glossed mouth. Instead, he raised her clasped hand toward his mouth. He licked the back of her hand before lowering it onto his lap.

Tricia tilted her head around Melanie's body to take in the scene. Chase bit back a smile.

He barely registered the rest of the proceedings. Francis was remanded into custody and Rachel was led inside. It was three minutes before 10:00 a.m. Skip Wilson strolled toward the defense table. Chase took that lull time to face Melanie.

"Let's go out, tonight," he said.

Melanie rolled her eyes and tugged her hand out of his grasp. Chase held on.

"I'll release you if you let us have our first date," he whispered. The first of many dates if Chase had his way. Judd and Nadine would be married and expecting their fourth child before Chase and Melanie's first date if he did not act. It was time to boot this romance into gear and out of neutral.

"Okay. Pick me up at seven," Melanie whispered.

"Deal." Chase released her hand.

Judge Wilkinson asked Rachel to enter her plea.

Her, "Not guilty," was followed with whispers but no uproar. Chase breathed a sigh of relief. Melanie's body trembled next to him and he looked over to see her crying.

Chase put his arms around her and Melanie leaned into his embrace. Tricia then rested her head on Melanie's arm. Chase stretched his hand to give Tricia's shoulder a light squeeze.

They held that position until the next case was called. Chase scuttled the women out into the hall. The waterworks exploded.

Chase uttered words of comfort as they cried.

"She looked so ... alone and scared." Tricia hiccupped as she signed and spoke.

"I can't bear to see her in handcuffs," Melanie said.

Chase made his way with the women toward the restroom. They withdrew from his arms and went inside to compose themselves.

While he waited, Chase pulled up YouTube and typed in Nadine's name in the search bar. There were dozens of clips posted online already. In the space of an hour, her outburst had gone viral.

He played the one with two hundred thousand views. Chase's mouth popped open when he saw the clip of Judd scooping Nadine in his arms. Nadine had gazed into Judd's face before cradling her head into his chest.

The gossip reporter's words made Chase's stomach clenched. *Nadine Ashton was seen exiting the courthouse in the arms of her* personal *Black Hulk. Forget about Francis. That kidnapping thief is going down. We all want to know, who is Judd Armstrong?*

17

"What are you doing going out with a cop?" Melanie glanced at her reflection in the bathroom mirror and plumped her lips with *Wet n Wild* Red-Dy or Not balm stain. "You know you don't date cops."

Yet she had been glued to Chase at court. His presence soothed her. She would not have made it without him earlier that day.

Dressed in a cream-colored chemise, Melanie walked over to her closet. She pulled out a red mini-dress and shimmied into it. Then she slipped her feet into black pumps before retrieving her sweater coat. It was a balmy 75 degrees but the weather could drop a good 15 degrees before the night was over.

Melanie returned to the bathroom and pulled her hair up into a messy bun. At 6:59, she saw her lights flash, which meant Chase had pressed the doorbell. Chase was punctual. She grabbed her purse and bustled to open the door.

Chase leaned against the door jam. In his blue shirt and tan khakis against those green eyes, Melanie swallowed to keep from drooling. It had been two weeks since she had seen Chase. Two weeks too long, her eyes told her.

"You look stunning," Chase said, moving closer.

Reading his lips made Melanie think of kissing. She wanted to taste them again. Melanie wondered if the searing kiss they had shared had been a fluke. There was only one way to find out. Chase must have read her thoughts because his eyes darkened.

"If you keep looking at me like that I'll ... Oh what the heck." Chase grabbed Melanie's head and pulled her against him. His lips met hers. Melanie accepted all Chase had to give. She closed her eyes, welcoming the sensations rocking her body. She could spend forever in Chase's arms and it would not be enough. That feeling scared but exhilarated her.

Then Chase broke the kiss. He tapped her lips. "I must do that again. But later." He stepped back and glanced at his watch. "We had better get going. I plunked some money into these last minute tickets and..." The rest of his words were lost as Chase lowered his head.

Melanie patted him on his chin.

Chase blushed. "I'm sorry. I said let's go because we're going to the Barbara B. Mann Theater in Fort Myers. I bought tickets to *The Phantom of the Opera*."

Melanie locked the door behind her. Her shoe slid on something. She tilted her heel and saw an envelope underneath. She knew without looking it was another letter from Janet. Melanie bent down and shoved it under her door.

When she rose, Melanie met Chase's curious gaze. "It's a letter from my mother," she found herself saying, although Melanie did not feel she owed Chase an explanation.

Chase crooked his head. "Are you ever going to read them?"

Melanie shook her head. "Let's not waste this beautiful night on that discussion." She walked over to Chase's vehicle and waited for him to open her door.

Chase let her inside and ran around the front to his side. When he was settled, Melanie tugged his sleeve. "You like musicals?"

"My mother did. When my brother and I were younger, we had to sit through *The Sound of Music*. I think I'm the only grown man who knows the lyrics and the lines to that film."

Melanie smiled. "I love anything involving the arts. I didn't know *The Phantom of the Opera* was on tour. I would have dragged Tricia with me. She hates watching musicals, says people breaking out in song at random moments is ridiculous."

Chase grinned. "I'll gladly be your partner." He tilted his head. "How do you keep up with the show considering there's music?"

Melanie closed her eyes. "I feel it. I can't explain it to you but the beat fills every part of me, from my feet all the way up to my heart. I love the dramatic scenes and the costumes." She opened her eyes, touched her heart, and smiled. "I'll enjoy every minute of the performance. I might not be able to hear it as you do but it still touches me."

Chase returned her smile. Melanie's heart flip-flopped. She liked the idea of Chase being her partner.

He turned on the car and backed out of the driveway. Soon they were on US 75. Chase drove at a fast but safe speed. He was a good driver. Melanie relaxed into her seat, knowing a conversation was not possible.

Melanie slanted her eyes toward Chase. She watched him navigate the two-lane highway, admiring the jut of his jaw and returning the occasional smile he flashed her way. When Chase reached over to take her hand in his, Melanie stiffened. The urge to remove her hand was strong. A part of her feared allowing Chase to get close to her. Another part of her knew there was no resisting.

Chase rubbed his thumb along the inside of Melanie's palm. Instantly, her heart rate increased. Go with the flow, she told herself.

Chase made the thirty-minute ride in twenty. By the time they pulled into the lot, Melanie was more than ready for another kiss. She willed herself to think of a Bible verse, do anything but stare at the gorgeous man opening her door.

Chase grasped her hand to help her out of the vehicle. Heat seared through her body. Melanie leaned into Chase and hugged him.

Chase withdrew slightly. He cupped her face in his hands. "I'm loving your first voluntary physical contact and believe me I could stay in this position for an eternity, but the show starts in five minutes."

Melanie scooted close. "I want to kiss you."

Chase's eyes darkened. "Now?"

Melanie nodded.

He chuckled. "I'll never get you women and your timing but I'm more than happy to comply." His tongue darted out to lick her lips.

Melanie captured his head in her hands. Closing her eyes, she kissed Chase with every ounce of passion she could muster.

Chase deepened the kiss.

Melanie.

Melanie heard the warning call from within and broke contact. She scurried across the lot to the entrance of the Barbara B. Mann Theater. Chase caught up to her.

"I had to get moving. You're going to make us late," she teased.

Chase turned Melanie to face him. "Me?" His eyes widened. "I make it a policy to grant a beautiful woman's wishes every chance I get."

They made their way through the queue and one of the attendants directed them to their seats in the lower mezzanine.

"You ran off like horses were chasing you," Chase commented, once they were settled.

Melanie knew she blushed. "I heard God talking to me. I knew I had to stop."

He squinted. "Heard? How can that be?"

Melanie shrugged. "God talks everybody's language, even mine. I feel Him. I know His voice."

Chase nodded, but Melanie knew he would never understand. God spoke to her like He did everyone

145

else. She knew it and *He* knew it. Melanie figured that was one of God's mysteries. She was not in a hurry to figure it out.

The curtains opened and the lights dimmed. Clutching Chase's hand, Melanie tuned her attention to the show.

***

Chase enjoyed watching Melanie's face throughout the performance. There were times where her eyes popped wide and her mouth hung open as she soaked up the scene unfolding before her.

If he had not known, there was no way Chase would peg Melanie as a deaf person. His admiration for her grew. She had a rough childhood but still embraced the whimsy of the arts. He watched as her eyes filled at the end of the performance.

Something in the back of his mind rose to the forefront. The letter. The cop in him questioned Melanie's actions. He wanted to ask her more about it but Chase did not want to spoil her good mood.

Maybe he should let her deal with her mother in her own way. Melanie had been doing fine without his interference for all these years. He needed to mind his business.

But, Chase could not let the matter rest.

They stopped at Bistro 41 to eat and Melanie rambled on about the opera. While she spoke, Chase visualized the letter. Melanie said she kept them in a drawer. How could she not be interested in reading them?

Chase covered his own curiosity with engaging conversation. He was proud his tongue had not betrayed him. It behaved until he pulled into Melanie's driveway.

"Thank you so much for tonight," Melanie said with warmth in her eyes.

"Are you going to invite me inside?" Chase asked.

Her eyes frosted. "You know better than to ask me that. It's close to midnight." Melanie opened the door and jumped out. She fumbled in her bag presumably to dig for her house keys.

Chase rushed out the vehicle and grabbed Melanie's hand. He made her look at him. "I want to see them," he said.

Melanie's brows furrowed. "What are you talking about? You're not making any sense. What do you want to see?"

"Your mother's letters. I think it's time you opened them."

18

Who did he think he was? Chase had overstepped his bounds. Melanie turned away from him. "I've got work in the morning. I'll call you," she said, through gritted teeth.

Chase rested a hand on her shoulder. He walked into her field of vision. "If you're secure with God and your family as you say, why are you scared to read them? How could a few letters from your mother hurt you?"

Melanie glared. "Janet's in my past. I have no desire to go back there."

Chase caressed her cheek with the back of his hand. "You're still in the past. Your closet scare is proof of that. Your past helped to shape your entire life. You can't run from it."

"You're being a nosy cop," Melanie said. "Now I'd better go before we ruin a really good night." She scooted around him and unlocked her door.

Chase's head popped into her view. He stood in front of her door and looked deep into her eyes. "Just think about it. Maybe those letters are not about you or for you. Maybe they are about her. Maybe your mother hasn't moved on and she's the one stuck in the past."

Melanie raised an eyebrow. "I'll think about it."

Chase gave her a quick peck on the cheek. "I know I'm intruding into your life but your mother's alive. I wish my mother were here. Every day I miss her. It's been three years and I haven't missed her any less. I'm glad she's with God but … I can't touch her or hold her. I'll never hear her voice." His sad eyes moved Melanie's heart.

"You will again, one day," Melanie whispered. She sniffed to keep the tears at bay. Chase's impassioned plea chipped at her resolve. Rhoda had been urging her to mend the bond with Janet. "I didn't have the kind of relationship with my mother that you had with yours. But, I promise to think about it—no, I'll pray on it. I'll let God lead me."

Chase nodded. "I'll pray as well. Thanks for not telling me off."

Melanie bit back a smile. "The thought had crossed my mind but I know you mean well, so …"

Chase tipped her chin and planted a tender kiss on her lips. Melanie ran her fingers in his hair. Desire raged through her as her body remembered Chase's expertise. It took her several seconds to realize he had ended the kiss.

"I can't wait until tomorrow so I can call you," Chase said before rushing off.

Melanie understood his hasty departure. If he stayed any longer, he would be inside her house and in her bed. Melanie wrinkled her nose. She had never disrespected her parents' home but the temptation of Chase's kisses was hard to resist.

Caught up in her thoughts, she realized Chase was waving her inside the house. She entered her home, locked the door, and kicked the pumps off her feet. Melanie eyed the envelope on the floor and picked it up.

It's time.

Melanie nodded. It was time. God was showing her in so many ways and it was time she took heed. She clutched the envelope to her chest and walked into her bedroom. She dropped to her knees and held the letter up to God.

"Lord, give me the strength and wisdom to deal with whatever's in here. I realize You're telling me to reach out to my mother. I don't know why but I'm going to trust You," Melanie prayed. "Heal Chase's heart as well, Lord. Thanks for bringing him into my life. I—I leave whatever this is between us in Your hands. In Jesus' name, Amen."

Melanie yawned and crept into her bed keeping the letter close. Armed with prayer, Melanie would reenter the battlefield of her past. Tomorrow. Tomorrow, she would make the first step toward reuniting with Janet.

A tear slid down her face. Melanie buried her face in the pillow. She realized she was not finished talking to God. "I blame her, Lord. I do. I lost my hearing because of Janet's alcohol and drug addiction. She let Uncle beat me and I'll never hear again. I don't know how to even ... *breathe.* The pain is so sharp. God help me," Melanie cried. Chase's face popped before her and she chuckled. "Lord, what a pushy man. Chase is acting like he's in love with me. I know love is a strong word. Isn't it too soon for all that?"

I have loved you from the moment I first knew you.

The verse from Jeremiah 1:5 came back to her. "Before I formed thee in the belly I knew thee..." Melanie smiled and closed her eyes. How good it felt to be loved by God.

The next morning, Melanie awakened to a calm peace. She made sure to put Janet's letter in her bag when she left for work. Throughout the day, Melanie's thoughts wandered to the letter.

It was a busier than usual Friday and Melanie was swamped with appointments and walk-ins. But the letter in her bag plagued her. By the time her work day ended, she had worked herself into a frenzy. Chase had texted her but her mind was too clouded to respond. Besides, a tiny part of her blamed him for barging into her life and making her feel things she was not ready for, yet. Melanie jumped into her car and drove to the dance studio.

She waved at the Hartman's before entering one of the empty studios. Melanie inserted Tasha Cobb's Grace CD in the player and chose track 7, *Break Every Chain*. Yes, this was the perfect song. Melanie needed freedom.

Melanie pushed her body hard as the words flowed through her mind. The vibrations flowed through her and guided her movements. As she twirled and twisted, God spoke to her.

He was ready. Ready to break the chains of the past. All she had to do was let Him. Yes. She could do that. Let God do it. Loose her from the bonds of the past so she could truly love someone. Someone like Chase.

When the song ended. Melanie rejoiced. Her chest heaved as she caught her breath and cooled down. Then she marched to her purse and retrieved the letter.

Melanie slid to the floor and tore open the envelope. She unfolded the paper. Her hands shook and sweat beads lined her upper lip. Janet's handwriting was a combination of print and script.

Hi, Lainey, it began. It's been years since she had been 'Lainey' to anyone. She kept reading.

This is my 129th letter to you. I can't tell if you read the others or not but I need somebody to write. This is an extra special day for me. I'm getting baptized tonight. I can hardly believe it. God wants me. At least that's what Pastor Ferguson keeps saying. He said it so much I started believing him. God's the only One who wants me anyways. I'm reading my Bible and Pastor Ferguson is real good at explaining scripture to me. It's nice knowing when I die I have some place better to go.

I sure wish I could see you. I try to imagine what you must look like. My beautiful baby girl. I wonder if you're married or if you've got kids. I love you, Lainey. Even if I never see you, again, I feel good knowing I did one thing right when I had you.

I love you,

Janet King.

Melanie read her mother's words three more times. She wept every time she read, *I try to imagine what you must look like.* She wiped her eyes and stood. A visual image of the other 128 letters shoved into her nightstand came into her mind. She had to read the other letters. A thirst filled her being. Melanie stuffed her clothes into her gym bag and rushed out the door.

She made the drive home in record time. Melanie

burst through her door and headed for the nightstand. She opened the drawer but it was stuck. There were too many letters in there.

Melanie wiggled it and tugged. She reached her hand into the drawer to pull out the envelopes caught in the groove. Then she pulled the drawer out with all her might. Letters flew all over the carpet and her bed, but Melanie did not care. She plopped the drawer on her bed.

Melanie ran her hands over the envelopes. They would take some time to organize. She shrugged and picked a random letter to read.

Melanie chose one dated February 11, 2014 and read. Then she chose another, and another. Melanie had no idea how long she read until she saw her mother standing by the door that led to her parent's section of the house.

"Melanie, do you want some chicken noodle soup?" Rhoda signed.

Melanie looked at her watch. She had not eaten since 11 that morning. "I'd love some, Mom. Come in."

Rhoda strolled inside. She scanned the mess from all the torn envelopes and smiled. "You're reading Janet's letters."

Melanie nodded. "Yes and I wished I had sooner. Janet has earned her GED and she's taking some classes online. She even told me about a preacher, Pastor Ferguson, who preached to her about God. Janet gave her life to God. She's sober."

Rhoda smiled. She spoke and signed, "That's wonderful news. Maybe God needed her behind bars to save her life."

"Before reading these letters, I would've thought that statement was far-fetched. But, now I know there's no limiting God."

"Are you going to write her back?" Rhoda asked.

Melanie scrunched her nose. "I think so but I want to finish reading her letters. I've read about 40 of them and my eyes are burning. My head is so full that I need to process and compose my thoughts." She tilted her head. "What do I say to the mother I haven't spoken to in years."

Rhoda's face held a tender expression. "I love you. That would be enough for me."

"Do you think I should see her?" Melanie asked.

Rhoda nodded. "I think you should. But when you're ready."

Melanie nodded.

"Come get some soup," Rhoda said. She stretched a hand. "Your stomach's growling."

Melanie patted her stomach and laughed. "Thanks for telling me. What does it sound like?" She remembered when Rhoda had to point out that flatulence had a sound not just a smell and chuckled.

"Like a lion's roar," Rhoda said.

Melanie shook her head. She had never heard a lion's roar.

Rhoda squinted her eyes and tapped her lips. "Like thunder."

Melanie raised her eyebrows. "I remember the sound of thunder and how loud it was. I guess I'd better eat then." She sniffed the air. "Hmm... My mouth's watering."

"Come, let me fix you a bowl." Rhoda placed an arm around Melanie's waist and ushered her into the kitchen.

Melanie plunked into the chair. Rhoda shared Melanie a generous portion of her homemade chicken soup. She used chicken breasts and added pumpkin to flavor the broth. Then Rhoda added dumplings, potato, and corn.

Melanie took a bite and moaned. "This is soooo good, Mom."

Rhoda wiped her hands on her apron and sat across from Melanie. "What made you decide to read the letters?"

Melanie scooped a spoonful of the broth in her mouth. Some of it dribbled down her chin. She grabbed a napkin. "It's not what, but who. It was Chase who urged me to read them."

Rhoda lifted a brow. "Chase?"

Melanie smiled. "The officer who arrested Rachel. We went on a date."

"You're dating a cop?" Rhoda asked. She knew all about Melanie's aversion to officers.

"Chase is different," she said, before dipping her head to eat more of her soup.

She saw Rhoda's hand tapping the table and looked up.

"When am I going to meet him?" Rhoda asked.

"Soon," Melanie said. "We only went out once. I'm not sure ..." Melanie trailed off. That was not quite true. "I like him but let me see where it goes."

Rhoda grinned. "You like him?"

"Chase is saved and he seems to be for real with his love for God." Melanie gushed. "He's also a good listener and he's so ... I can't put it into words, but being around him brightens my day." Melanie felt her face warm.

She saw Rhoda clapping her hands. "I'm happy for you. It sounds like you're in love, again. You're filling me with good news today, Melanie. It feels good to see answered prayers in action. Two out of three isn't bad. I'll wait on God to do the rest. Bring your man by for dinner." Rhoda did a praise dance.

"Love might be a strong word. I just met him." Melanie ducked her head to hide her face. She knew the truth was in her eyes. But, she was scared. The last man she had brought home was her fiancé. Her head popped up. "Wait. What do you mean by two out of three?"

"You caught that." Rhoda chuckled. "I've been praying for you to open your heart to your mother. I've been praying for you to find a man. And ... I've been praying you'll return to your real career—dancing."

Melanie gritted her teeth. "Mom, leave the dancing alone. I'm not leaving Port Charlotte. I do dance. In fact, Pastor asked me to do a special dance next Saturday in church."

Rhoda nodded. "That's not enough. Dance is your

ministry. Your passion. You've got to be all in not just a part-time participant."

"I'm all into what I'm doing now. Trust me, it's enough." Even as she said the words, Melanie knew she was lying.

Her mother knew it, too. Rhoda pursed her lips. "I'll keep praying."

Melanie finished her bowl of soup and stood. "You can pray all you want. Don't mean you'll get what you ask for."

"It's working so far," Rhoda said.

"I've been praying for the opposite." Melanie held her hands on her hips. "We'll see who wins the prayer battle."

Rhoda tapped Melanie's chin. "You have so much to learn. It's not a battle if it's already done."

19

"Nadine won't see me or take my calls. It's been a week and I'm going nuts," Judd raged.

Chase and Judd exited the precinct Thursday evening, a little after five o'clock. Their shift had just ended.

"Since that picture of me carrying her out of the courthouse hit the Internet, she's avoided me like I'm contagious," Judd continued.

"And, she should." Chase walked in step with Judd. They headed towards Judd's patrol car.

Judd glared. "What do you mean, she should?"

Chase felt his cell phone vibrate. It was a text from Melanie. Chase and Melanie had a dinner and movie date that evening.

DON'T GET OUT THE CAR. JUST FLASH YOUR LIGHTS.

OK, he texted back, then continued his conversation with Judd.

"You shouldn't be involved with Nadine and you know it. She's emotional. Her son was kidnapped and her husband cheated on her. She's not making rational decisions right now."

"Nadine is justified. Francis messed about on her first."

"Adultery is never right. No matter the cause. God's standards never change. She's a married woman and off limits," Chase said.

Judd lowered his eyes. "You're right. My mother would box my ears if she knew. I've never touched a married woman. But, Nadine—"

Chase held a hand up. "No buts. Stay away from her. If you really want to help her, you'll pray for her."

Judd nodded. "I've been meaning to get back into church."

Chase smirked. "You've been saying that for ages. Waiting on you to come with me to church is like waiting on water to boil."

Judd lifted a chin. "I tell you what. I'll be there this Saturday."

"I'll believe it when I see it, my friend. In the meantime, cheer up. Watch the game for the both of us tonight."

"Patriots all the way," Judd said before opening his car door.

Chase threw a fist in the air. He drove home, showered and changed, then headed over to pick up Melanie.

He flashed the lights a couple times before Melanie stepped outside. Chase's throat went dry. Melanie was dressed in fitted blue jeans tucked inside thigh high boots. Her black sweater and bedazzled cowboy hat completed her ensemble. Chase would have whistled

159

but he knew she would not hear him.

Melanie walked with the poise of a supermodel.

Chase got out the car to open the passenger door for Melanie. He resisted the corny, "Howdy, partner," and said, "You look amazing."

She batted her lashes. "Thank you." Melanie kissed Chase on the cheek, then got in the car.

Chase ran around to the driver's side of the car and got in.

"Where are we eating?" she asked. "I'm starving."

"I was thinking we could go to Carrabba's. All the movies start at about seven, so we have plenty of time."

"I love Carrabba's. Good choice. Let's get going," Melanie said.

Chase loved the smell of vanilla wafting up to his nose. He would not mind feasting on her instead.

You need to be feasting on your Bible.

Chase accepted the rebuke and put the car in gear. Once they got to Carrabba's Italian Grill, Chase and Melanie were seated in a corner by the window. Chase helped Melanie into one of the wooden chairs before taking his own seat.

"It's pretty scanty in here," Melanie observed.

Chase looked around. There were two other couples a few tables down. "All the better. We'll get served fast."

A waitress approached. "Welcome to Carrabba's. I'm Amanda. Can I start you with something to drink and an appetizer?"

"I'll get water. I'm ready to order, if you are," Melanie said to Chase.

"I'll have water as well, and I do know what I want." Chase smiled at the waitress. "I'll have the Mezzaluna."

Amanda nodded then looked at Melanie.

"I'll have the Fettuccine Carrabba," Melanie said.

Amanda scribbled their order on her notepad and collected the menus. "I'll put the order in and I'll be back with your waters."

"Somebody is hungry," Chase teased.

Melanie nodded. "I skipped lunch today. Today was one of those days where everybody, their uncle, and their grandma came in for service."

Chase laughed.

"Then I went to visit Rachel."

Chase kept his tone neutral. "How is she doing?"

"She looks awful," Melanie said. "She's lost a lot of weight and she was in low spirits. I prayed with her and encouraged her as best I could, but ..."

"Jail's not an easy place," Chase said as the waitress came with their waters and some complimentary Italian rolls.

"I just wish I could do more to help." Melanie's shoulders sagged.

"You are helping. You're praying for her." He thought of Judd. "Sometimes, that's all you can do for your friends. Pray for them and love them."

Melanie sipped her water. "I read Janet's letters."

Chase's eyes widened. "All of them? That's great. Why didn't you tell me sooner?"

"I couldn't until I was finish reading all 129 of them. I wasn't sure what my next move would be but I've decided to visit her. According to Janet's letters, she's a changed woman. Mom did a praise dance when I told her. She's been at me for years to reach out to Janet. She says it's answered prayer."

Chase bit into one of the Italian rolls. "I'm glad you're going to see your biological mother. I was praying about it as well. Where is she?" He knew Janet was not housed in Charlotte County.

"She's in Tampa," Melanie said. She picked up a roll and tore off a small piece. "I was hoping you'd come with me. I plan to go next Sunday."

Chase reached across the table to touch her hand. "Of course, I'll come. I'm touched you'd ask me."

Her eyes were warm. "I want you with me."

Her words melted over Chase's heart like snow under the sun. "Melanie, I ..." He bent his head. The words, "I love you," were on the tip of his tongue.

Melanie leaned in. "I'm sorry you lowered your head. What did you say?"

Chase's eyes met her expectant ones. He knew she knew what he wanted to say but he did not want to scare her off. "I wanted to ask what movie you wanted to see."

Melanie's eyes dimmed with disappointment but Chase planted a smile on his face. The awkward moment hung between them. Chase was glad to see Amanda appear with their steaming plates of food.

Chase took Melanie's hand. "Lord, we thank you for this meal You've provided. Remove all impurities so that it will enrich us. We pray this prayer in Jesus' name. Amen."

Melanie twirled her fettuccine around her fork and scooped it into her mouth. Some of the sauce was on the side of her mouth. Chase reached over and wiped the sauce away with his finger. Then he sucked his finger.

"I'll have to try this next time," Chase said.

Melanie's gaze was pinned on him. "That was hot what you just did."

Chase grinned. "When we're married, I'll use chocolate." He ate some of his Mezzaluna. His taste buds welcomed the burst of ricotta cheese and tomato cream sauce. "Hmmm. This is good."

"I want to see *Selma*."

Chase eyes widened at Melanie's words.

Her eyes held a challenge. Chase thought of the Oscar worthy movie depicting Dr. Martin Luther King's epic walk across the bridge. He opened his cell phone and pulled up the theater app to check show times. "The next show starts at 7:30, so we'll make it."

Melanie raised a brow. "You don't have a problem watching that with me?"

Chase shook his head. "Why should I?"

"Well, it deals with race issues."

"And?"

"Doesn't it make you uncomfortable?"

Chase shook his head. "No. I'm not responsible for the actions of an entire race. I'm only answerable for what I do. Besides, you don't know, if I were born back then, I could've been one of the people walking with Dr. King."

Melanie nodded. "I didn't think of that."

Chase touched her cheek. "So, we'll go see *Selma*."

"I'll wait for the DVD and watch it at home," Melanie said. "I only chose that because I wanted to see what you would say. Let's go see *The Boy Next Door* instead. I love Jennifer Lopez."

Chase narrowed his eyes. "You don't have to test me like that. Melanie, I'm quite aware that when society sees us, they see race first. With all the mess out there in the news with trigger-happy cops, I have to counteract that stereotype every day. Cops have a bad rep. When I'm on the road, I'm doing my job. Period." He gestured between them. "But when I look at you, all I see is a beautiful woman." His voice deepened. "A woman I can't wait to see every day. I'm sure I'll feel that way ten years from now."

Melanie's eyes glistened. "What are you saying?"

Chase reached for her hand. "Can't you tell? You must see how I feel about you? Melanie, I—"

Her phone vibrated. She looked to see who was calling. "That's my mom. I've got to take this." She swiped the answer button. "Mom?"

Chase watched as her smile froze. He heard Rhoda's voice but the volume was too low for him to hear from across the table.

"What's happened?" she asked. Her face lost all of its color. "Oh, no. I'll be there." Melanie ended the call and clutched her chest. "We have to go to the hospital. Right now."

Chase jumped to his feet but she was speeding toward the front door. He tossed sixty dollars on the table and rushed after Melanie.

20

"She'll be on bed rest for the rest of her pregnancy, but thank God, Tricia's all right," Melanie said, coming out to the Fawcett Hospital emergency room wait area where Chase sat waiting. She had rushed inside while Chase parked his Jeep.

Chase heaved a sigh of relief. "I'm glad to hear your sister and her baby are okay."

"You can come back if you want," Melanie said. "My parents would like to meet you."

"Now? Are you sure? I want to meet them but this is not how I envisioned it? I wanted to—"

Melanie held out her hand, stilling Chase's comment. "Come meet my parents."

Chase wiped his sweaty palms on his jeans. "Do you have any gum? I can't meet them with questionable breath."

Melanie laughed. To Chase, it was a sweet sound. He wished she could hear it. She rummaged into her purse and pulled out a stick of gum. Chase plopped it into his mouth. Then he held out a hand. When Melanie clasped her hand in his, Chase felt his heart shift. It was at that moment he acknowledged he was in love with Melanie. He never wanted to let her go.

The attendant on duty unlocked the door so they could go back into patient care. Melanie drew back the curtain and they entered the room. Tricia was propped up on the bed with a fetal monitor and blood pressure monitor attached.

"Chase, meet Gary and Rhoda Benson, my parents," Melanie said, going over to stand between them.

Chase held out a hand and shook Gary's. Rhoda gave him a hug. Chase returned the shorter woman's embrace.

"I'm so glad to meet you, Chase," Rhoda said, pulling away. "Melanie has been beaming and now I know why. You're one handsome man."

Chase knew his face warmed. "Thank you. It's a pleasure meeting both of you."

Melanie rolled her eyes. "Trust Mom to embarrass me," she spoke and signed.

Tricia spoke up. "Nice seeing you again, Chase. I hope it will be under better circumstances next time."

Chase nodded. "Take it easy." A flash of Melanie's tummy rounded with his child entered his mind. How he would like that. Chase looked Melanie's way. She was fussing.

"You must come over for dinner," Rhoda said, turning his attention away from Melanie.

Gary shook his head. "Give the young man a moment to breathe, Rhoda. Don't be pushy." He curled an arm about Melanie's waist. Melanie closed her eyes and smiled.

So, she's a Daddy's girl, Chase observed.

"I'd love to come to dinner," Chase said to Rhoda. "Just let me know the date and time."

A doctor and nurse entered the small area. "Let's see how our patient's doing."

Chase took that as his exit cue. "I'd better be going."

Melanie stepped forward. "I'll walk you out."

From the corner of her eye, Melanie saw Tricia waving her hands. She turned to face her sister.

"Go on with Chase." Tricia rubbed her tummy. "This little guy's going to be just fine. Mom and Dad will stay with me until Emory arrives."

Melanie bit her lip. "I don't know if …"

"Go," Tricia urged. "Nothing's going to happen. Mom prayed so hard I know God heard her loud and clear."

After another reluctant nod, Melanie ambled over to where Chase stood. Once again they joined hands.

"Call me if there's any change," Melanie said.

"If you'd step outside for a minute, we just have to make sure Mrs. Yang and baby are okay," the doctor said.

Her parents stepped out in the hallway with Melanie and Chase. The nurse pulled the curtain close.

"Chase, are you saved?" Rhoda asked and signed.

"Rhoda! This is not the time to question Chase about his personal beliefs. At least wait until you've fattened him up," Gary joked.

"Yes, I am. I accepted Christ three years ago and that's the best decision I've ever made." He squeezed Melanie's hand. "The second was going out with your daughter."

Rhoda touched her chest. "Oh, I like you," she whispered, a little choked up. "Come over next Thursday and we'll talk some more." Rhoda signed her words as well so Melanie could hear.

"More like an inquisition," Gary said.

"Mom, lay off," Melanie said. She tugged Chase away from her parents. 'See you later." They walked outside the emergency room. "I'm sorry you had to go through that just now. I would apologize for my mother, but that's who she is. She's bound to ask you more outrageous questions next week."

Chase laughed. "I don't mind. Your mother can ask me anything she wants. I'm willing to face the *inquisition* for you."

Melanie blushed.

As they stood by the automatic doors of the emergency entrance, Chase could hold his words no longer. He turned Melanie toward him and said, "I love you, Melanie."

She barely met his eyes. "I care about you, too, Chase."

Chase bit back his disappointment. He tells a girl he loves her and she says she cares for him. He pulled Melanie close and kissed her. Her body melted into his and her breathing labored. Chase had his answer. Her body did not lie. He broke the kiss and look into Melanie's eyes. What he saw stole his breath. She loved him but she was scared. Scared of feeling. He could understand that as he loved Melanie with an intensity he found hard to put into words. He could wait for the words.

"Chase," she spoke his name with a raspy breath.

He put a finger over her lips. "I need you to meet my father," he said.

Melanie released a shaky laugh and fiddled with her sweater. "Turnabout, huh?"

"The last time I took a woman home was when my mother was alive. I said the next woman I take home would be the one I plan to marry."

Melanie's eyes widened. Chase cracked up at the panic in her eyes. "Don't worry, I have no plans of asking you right now. But, I'm putting you on notice so you know my future plans."

"I ... I ..." Melanie gulped.

Chase held his smile and walked to his Jeep. His butterfly was a little freaked out. That was okay by him. Melanie lingered a few steps behind. Her arms were folded about her. In time, his butterfly would land. And, he would have her just where he wanted her. His bed.

21

"Thanks for coming with me," Melanie said to Chase that Sunday. They had passed through security and had already been screened. She was dressed in an *Aeropostale* white tee shirt and blue jeans with sneakers. She had a white cover up in case it was cold inside the jailhouse.

"I would have come even if you didn't ask me anyway," he said. Chase was also dressed in jeans and wore a green long-sleeved tee.

"I wonder if my mother will recognize me," Melanie signed.

Chase shook his head. "I only understood a couple words. Your hands moved too fast."

"I'm sorry," Melanie said. "When I get nervous, I forget you can't sign."

"Yet," he said, lifting a finger. "I've been taking lessons."

"The best way to learn is by doing," she spoke and signed.

She was pleased when Chase repeated her hand movements. Melanie appreciated his effort.

"From now on we will communicate by signing and speaking."

Chase nodded. "Good idea. Although I love watching your eyes on my lips."

Melanie jabbed him in the ribs and laughed. "You're a trip." She reached up to touch his cheek. "Thanks for making me laugh. I was nervous until now."

"I hope to make you laugh every day."

Melanie broke eye contact. Chase had these comebacks that made her feel so special. There were about ten other people in the holding area. The guard escorted them into the visiting room. It had the bare necessities. Bolted-down tables that had seen better days and rickety chairs. Melanie resisted the urge to scratch. She thought of her purse in Chase's Jeep, which had her tangerine-scented hand sanitizer and moaned. She hated this place and the moldy, rusty smell. Melanie wrinkled her nose. Surely their taxes provided more livable accommodations than this. She gripped Chase's hand.

Chase led her to an empty table in the corner. They sat next to each other with their backs against the wall. From their vantage point, Melanie would see when Janet arrived.

Chase rested an arm behind her chair. To Melanie, he looked composed but alert.

Melanie's stomach knotted. Her *Secret* deodorant was working over-time. If nervousness had a scent, she would be it.

Then Janet approached. Melanie's throat went dry. Unbidden, tears filled her eyes. She looked at the mother she had not seen in 22 years.

Janet scanned the room before her eyes rested on Melanie's. Melanie's heart leapt as Janet's eyes widened with recognition. Janet weaved through the other tables until she stood by the tables. The two connected. Janet ambled over in their direction.

Janet held her arms open though there was no physical contact allowed. "My beautiful daughter." The two connected. Melanie wiped her face and sat across from them. "Lainey," she said. "I can't believe you came."

Melanie signed and spoke. "I go by Melanie. It's good seeing you."

"I'm grateful you decided to visit me. When I got your note, I cried for two days straight," Janet said. "I see you read lips. I'm fixing to take some sign language classes."

Melanie nodded. Her shoulders tensed. She was deaf because of Janet's neglect. The urge to lash out surfaced but Melanie squelched it down. Bitterness had no place here. "You look great," she said.

Janet laughed. "Girl, don't lie to me. Drugs and alcohol did a number on me. The only thing tight on me is this dark skin. Everything else needs fixing."

Melanie stared. Janet's self-assessment was spot on. Her skin shone. However, she was missing a couple of teeth. Her once luxurious hair had thinned and she was smaller than Melanie remembered. But, Melanie had been five years old so her memory was murky.

Janet's curious eyes sought out Chase's. "Is that your bodyguard?" she asked.

"No, Chase is my ... friend."

Chase waved in greeting. He angled his body so Melanie could see him. "I'm hoping to be her fiancé one day."

"You're bold," Janet said.

Chase nodded. "It's nice meeting you. Now, I'm going to give you some time with your daughter." He stood.

Melanie missed his presence already. "You don't have to go," she said.

"No, you need time to bond."

When he was out of earshot, Janet said, "I'm glad to have you to myself a little."

Melanie squirmed. She didn't know what to say or how to act. If it were Rhoda, she would have been talking up a storm but her history with Janet was not pleasant. Maybe it was time to start better memories. She hunched her shoulders. "What do you want to know about me?" she asked.

"Anything you want to tell me," Janet said. "But first, I've got something to say to you. I'm sorry. Lainey, I'm sorry for not protecting you. I was your mother. I brought you into this world healthy and happy. I should've done everything in my power to keep you that way."

Melanie choked up. She needed Janet's words. "What about my father? Where was he?"

Janet shook her head. "I don't know who he is. I … I did a lot of things I wasn't proud of to score drugs. He could have been Hispanic or white or Indian. I have no idea."

Melanie swallowed the bile that threatened to spew. She closed her eyes and prayed on the inside. *Lord, this is tough to hear. I don't know if I can continue this reunion.*

I'm here. God breathed the words into her spirit, calming her.

Melanie felt the table vibrate. Janet was tapping the table. Melanie lifted her head. Janet's face was flushed from tears. "I'm so ashamed to tell you that but I won't lie to you."

"Thanks for being honest. I'm glad you're clean and sober now." Melanie gulped. "Do you have any more children?"

Janet's gaze shifted before she jutted her chin. "I had another child. A son but he died a month after he was born. Low birth weight. It's for the best as he was addicted to heroin. I wasn't able to keep sober like I was with you."

Lord, this is too much. Melanie turned away. She wished Chase had not left her alone with Janet. She wanted to scream and hurl but Melanie was not about to show out in jail.

I am with you.

Gathering her courage, Melanie turned around. Janet was humped over on the table. Her body shook. Melanie hated to witness the other woman's breakdown. But, she had to ask the tough questions before they could move forward. If there was a moving forward.

Melanie tapped the table.

Janet's head popped up. Her face looked ravaged

with pain. "I knew I would have to answer for my dirt one day. I didn't know it would feel like this," she said. "I feel like a knife is twisting my insides. I see the disgust on your face and I ..." She shook her head. "Maybe this was a bad idea. I've done too much."

"God has forgiven you." Melanie's eyes widened at her words. Where had those words come from? "God has forgiven me for many things. I can forgive you."

Janet cupped her mouth. "Oh, God. I don't deserve it."

One of the guards on duty brought them tissues. Thank goodness. Melanie and Janet blew their noses. They pulled more tissues and dabbed at the corner of their eyes.

Melanie straightened. "That's the power of forgiveness. We never deserve it. I can't hold anything you've done over your head. I was blessed with good parents who took me into their heart and home. They gave me so much love, I have plenty to share with you."

Janet fell apart at Melanie's words. "I'm glad you had them. I'm glad you've got your life together. I'm working on getting my act together so one day you can be proud of me."

Melanie's lip trembled. She wanted to be proud of Janet as well. "I'm proud you accepted God as your savior. He's all you need."

"God has changed my life. I'm clean and I'll be getting out in a few months. And, when I do, I won't be coming back. Ever."

"Amen," Melanie said. "I believe you."

Eyes like her own looked at her. "Do you?"

Melanie nodded. "We have that in common. I try not to say anything I don't mean."

"Can we stay in touch?" Janet asked.

"Yes. I want you in my life."

"Good. I hope that means you'll invite me to your wedding."

Melanie's brow furrowed. "Chase and I ... we're not engaged."

"You will be," Janet said. "I saw that man's face. He's in love with you. Just don't get married before I get out."

***

From her passenger seat, Melanie eyed the mile marker 223 and sighed.

Chase tapped her arm and Melanie turned to look at him. "You've been quiet the entire drive."

They were near the Ellenton shops exit on I-75.

"I was thinking about my conversation with Janet," Melanie said. "Some of the things she told me hurt. Like how I could have had a brother, but he was born addicted to heroin. And he died. He didn't even have a chance."

Chase rubbed her arm.

"Janet doesn't know who my father is," Melanie continued. "It makes me feel weird. Incomplete. My father is a nameless face."

Chase faced her. "You do know your father." He pointed heavenward. "God has taken you into His hands. He's the best father you could have."

"That's not the same." Melanie peered out the window, ending the conversation.

Chase pulled over on the curb.

"Are you crazy? We're on a major highway," she yelled.

"I know what I'm doing. I don't want you tuning me out when you feel like it. That is not going to happen."

Melanie exploded. "You know your father. You know his face and what he looks like. So save the platitude about God being my father. I know that. I don't need you patronizing me."

Chase got into her face. "You want me to feel sorry for you? Well I don't. You've got more than most women I know. You're beautiful. You have a body most women would kill to have. You have this fancy job and you drive a fancy car. So, I don't feel sorry for you. I think you're being ungrateful."

Melanie's neck snapped from side to side. "Is this how you speak to someone you claim to love? If so, you can keep it." She gathered her cover up around her needing that layer of protection.

Chase gripped the steering wheel. His chest heaved. Then he faced her. "I'm telling you the truth because I love you. I'm in love with you but that doesn't mean I'm going to lie flat as a pancake and let you walk over me. It doesn't mean I'm not going to tell you about yourself. If your breath stinks, I'm going to tell you because that's what love is about. Telling the ugly truth."

Melanie squinted. "Flat as a pancake."

He shrugged. "One of Judd's analogies."

She relaxed her shoulders. "Why are we fighting?"

"I don't know. I think you're trying to push me away." Chase's eyes held a tinge of sadness.

His accusation rang true. Starting a fight was her way of creating a wedge between them. Janet's assumption that they would get married frightened her. But being frightened was no excuse for losing her temper.

A truck whizzed by shaking the car. Chase started up the engine. Melanie tapped his arm. "I told my mom your testimony of how you got saved. I hope you don't mind my sharing. Mom said the same thing to me. She thinks I'm afraid to get hurt. Chase, don't leave even if it seems I'm pushing you away. Give me time."

"I don't mind you telling my truth, especially to your mother. I told my father about you. I'm trying, butterfly, to give you time because I know we're moving fast. But you know how to test a man's patience. Did you ask Janet about Uncle?"

Did he just call me Butterfly? Melanie shook her head. "I didn't have the guts to ask after all Janet dumped on me." Her shoulders slumped. "I'm sorry for my outburst. Things are going so well between us I have to pinch myself. It's like it's going too well. It's all sunshine now and I'm looking for the rain clouds."

179

Chase's eyes softened. "If the rain comes, I'll get you an umbrella. That's my job. But for now, relax and bask in the sunshine. It's okay to be happy."

"I don't know how," Melanie whispered. Tears glistened. "I'm scared that the minute I open myself then something bad will happen. I can't drop my guard."

"That's no way to live," Chase said. "When I lost my mother and brother, it hurt me to the core. I didn't know how I would live the rest of my life without them. I wished it were my father who had died. But God knew my mother and Vincent were His and He had plans. My father changed after that day. He became a believer and a new man. I, too, met Christ. I now believe nothing just happens. God has a way of working everything into something good." He smiled. "Like that day in January when I pulled you over. I'm not a patrol cop. I work in the Major Crimes unit. But God allowed our paths to cross because I was meant to meet you. God brought us together. I'm sure of that."

Another truck blew past shaking the car. Chase put the Jeep in gear and put on his indicator. "I've got to get off this curb and get you home safe."

Melanie let him drive while she pondered his words. She was jealous of Chase's optimism. She closed her eyes and admitted some truths to herself. She was afraid to love him. She felt the minute she told Chase she loved him, she would lose him. Melanie knew what she had to do.

Without opening her eyes, she said, "Take me to the studio. I need to dance."

22

"I shouldn't have come at her like that. I should've listened and kept my opinions to myself. Why did I open my mouth?" Chase mumbled under his breath, though Melanie could not hear him.

Chase drove in misery to the studio. He stole several glances at Melanie but she had her eyes closed. He did not know what she was thinking. His heart ached.

He pulled into the empty lot. Melanie jumped out of the car and rushed to open the door. Chase's shoulders lifted when he saw Melanie leave the door open. He walked to the same room he had watched her danced before.

She had kicked off her sneakers in the hall and her jeans were tossed on the floor. His eyes widened and his heart rate increased.

Chase poked his head through the door. His feet encountered her tee shirt. He heard the subtle tune of Elvis Presley's *Fool Rush In* fill the room. Where was the music coming from? Chase entered the empty space and looked around. Where was Melanie?

Chase stood in the center of the floor as the music swirled around him.

Then Melanie sailed into the room. Chase's breath caught. She was a vision in an ice blue leotard and swirling skirt. She flew toward him with the grace of a swan. He swallowed.

Melanie propped a leg around him. Then in a bold move, she pushed him away and got caught up in the dance. Chase watched her whirl around the room. He took out his phone and snapped several shots before pushing the phone into his pocket. He could not take his eyes off her. Melanie's fluidity and grace mesmerized him.

When the words, "I can't help falling in love with you," played for a second time, Melanie lip-synched the words. How she knew when to say them would remain a mystery. With each word, she floated toward him.

Chase knew she told him her feelings the best way she could. Through dance. His chest swelled. "I love you, too," he mouthed back.

Melanie held her arms open. Chase clasped her hands and moved with her. "I don't know the steps," he said.

She placed a finger on his lips. "Just move with your heart. Keep your eyes on me. Trust me."

Chase nodded. With his eyes on hers, he coordinated his step with hers. With each step, his trust grew. She led him around the room and Chase followed her lead. They kept their eyes pinned on each other and their hands joined. In all his life, Chase had never experienced such a romantic moment.

They danced together never losing contact until the song ended. Chase chest heaved as he strove to catch his breath. He released a breath of air, but Melanie opened her mouth, captured it, and pressed her lips to his.

She kissed Chase with so much passion, he felt off kilter. When she broke the kiss, Chase held her face with both his hands. "Thank you for the dance."

"Thank you for trusting me," she said. Then she squared her shoulders. "I love you. I want to be happy. See where this goes."

Chase smiled. "I love you, too. Thanks for trusting me with your heart."

"It's yours, as long as you want it." Melanie laughed. "And to think I said I would never date a cop. Not after Uncle."

Chase's eyes widened. "Uncle was a cop?"

She nodded.

Chase hugged her. Now he understood. If an officer of the law had beaten him to the point where he lost his hearing, he would stay away from them. Chase kissed the top of Melanie's head. No one would ever hurt her again, he vowed. Not while he had breath in his body. He heard a loud gargling sound and pulled back.

"Let's get out of here." Chase pointed to Melanie's stomach. "Your tummy's rumbling."

She patted her midriff. "Thanks for telling me. I'm not surprised. I'm starving. The bagel this morning was not enough. Let me get changed and lock up. Then we can figure out where we want to eat."

"I know where we can go. Let me make a phone

call."

With trust in her eyes, Melanie nodded. She blew him an air kiss and scooped up her clothes to change.

Chase pulled out his phone. "Hey, Dad. Are you up to lunch guests? Put some fish in the fryer. I'm bringing Melanie to meet you. I want you to meet my future wife."

***

"What if he doesn't like me?" Melanie asked.

"My father is going to love you. You're worried over nothing," Chase said. Melanie had fretted the entire thirteen minutes it took him to drive from the studio to Ted's house.

She leaned against his Jeep wringing her hands. Chase captured her hands and kissed them. They walked up to his childhood home. Chase opened the screen door. The front door was unlocked so they went inside.

"Dad? We're here," he called out.

He watched Melanie's curious gaze as she scanned the room. She wandered over to the wall unit where most of his handiwork was displayed.

"These are beautiful," she spoke and signed.

Chase's chest puffed with pride. "I made them." She turned back to admire the rest of the pieces.

His father walked in holding a large platter with

three large red snappers. "I just finished cleaning and seasoning these. I'll fry them outside."

"Dad, she can't hear you," he said, pointing toward Melanie.

"Oh, yes. Sorry, I forgot. Bring her outside," he said, going out to the lanai.

Chase went over to tap Melanie on the shoulder. "Come meet my dad."

She took his hand and Chase led her outside. "Melanie, I'd like you to meet Lieutenant Theodore Lawson. My father."

Melanie smiled. "It's nice to meet you, sir."

Ted rested the platter on the small table. Then he walked toward Melanie with an extended hand.

Suddenly, Melanie's body curled into Chase and she gripped his shirt.

"Uncle! Uncle!" she screamed, covering her ears.

Chase froze. *Uncle?* Goose bumps rose on his flesh.

Ted shook his head. He dropped his hand. Shock was written all over his face. "What's going on?" he asked.

"Why did you bring me here?" Melanie lifted terrified eyes to look at Chase. Her body shivered and she looked ghost-pale. "Is this some sick joke?"

"What are you talking about?" Chase asked.

His father looked puzzled. He took a step toward Melanie.

She held up a hand. "Don't touch me. Don't come

near me." With that, she jerked out of Chase's arms and sped through the house.

"I'll call you," Chase yelled to his father before racing after Melanie. She moved with the speed of a deer and could be halfway down the block already.

Chase tore through the screen door and stopped short. Melanie's body was folded over the hood of his Jeep. Her shoulders shook from the intensity of her crying. Her wails whipped at his heart. He staggered over to where she was and leaned into her.

Melanie twisted her body and clung to him. Chase stroked her hair. Had she screamed at him, he would have felt better. But, the woman in his arms trembled from head to toe.

She soaked his shirt with her tears. "Uncle. Uncle," she sobbed. "He beat me. He made them take my mama from me."

Chase looked to see his father standing by the front door. Chase shook his head. Ted's face fell but he went back inside. It took Chase another ten minutes before Melanie released him. He gently deposited her into his Jeep and drove her home.

For the entire drive, Melanie huddled into the corner as far away from him as possible. Chase dared not question her about Uncle. He prayed this was all a misunderstanding. As long as he lived, Chase would never forget Melanie's scream or the stark fear on her face.

Could my father... ?

No. Chase shook his head. Ted was not that monster. There had to be some other explanation. He swerved into her driveway and went to the front of the house to ring the doorbell.

Gary answered the door.

"Come, quick. It's Melanie," Chase said. He sprinted back to his Jeep, afraid to leave Melanie alone too long.

Gary was right behind him. "What's wrong? Did Janet upset her?"

"I wish it were that. She thinks my father is Uncle," was all Chase could say.

Gary went to the passenger side and opened the door. Melanie rolled into her father's arms. Chase saw Gary struggle to hold her. Chase went over and swung Melanie into his arms.

Gary crooked his head and Chase followed him into the house. "Rhoda's at Tricia's house," he said. "Put her on the couch."

Chase deposited Melanie on the floral sofa. He stroked her face but she shuttered her eyes and closed him out. His heart ached. Melanie did not want to look at him.

Gary came over and tapped his shoulder. "You should go. I'll see to her. Rhoda will be home, soon."

"But …"

"Go, son. I need to talk to my daughter. She needs her family right now."

Gary's words pierced his very soul. "She is my family," he croaked. "I love her. I want to spend the rest of my life with her."

"Then pray for her." Gary's tone was firm but his eyes were filled with compassion.

Melanie started to cry again. The couch muffled her tears but seeing her so distraught broke Chase's spirit.

Gary went over to his daughter.

"Is Chase gone?" she asked. "I don't think I can bear to look at him. Uncle. Uncle. *Uncle* is his father."

Gary waved him out. Chase sagged. His cell phone vibrated. Chase saw Ted's face appear on the screen.

Rage blinded his good sense. He stomped outside the Benson's home to answer the phone. "How much more are you going to take from me?" he snarled into the phone. "Because of you I lost my mother and brother. And now I lost the woman I loved."

"Son, let me—"

"Is it true?" he interrupted. "Are you Uncle? That's all I want to know."

"I ..."

"Is it true?" he yelled.

"I—I don't know. Son, give me a chance—"

Chase squinted against the sun. How could he not know? "No! No more chances. I looked up to you. I thought you were a hero. But, you're nothing but a monster. A monster. I told you about Melanie and how she lost her hearing and you said whoever hurt a child should be hanged. Well, get the noose, Dad. Get the noose!"

188

23

Rhoda entered Melanie's suite holding a tray with tea, a muffin, and half a grapefruit. "Aren't you going to work today?"

Melanie shook her head. She pulled herself up in a sitting position. Her hair was uncombed and her eyes were bloodshot. "Thanks, Mom." Her stomach was filled from hurt but Melanie took a small bite of the muffin. "I'm not going back. I sent Nancy my two-weeks notice. Then I put in for my vacation days. I have at least three months so I'm not worried."

"How could you quit like that?" Rhoda perched on the bed. "That wasn't professional. You might not get a reference."

Melanie shrugged. "I don't care. Wasn't that what you've been telling me to do for months?"

"I said to pursue your dreams, but I wasn't advocating you up and quitting like this," Rhoda said. "I didn't think being a banker satisfied you. I'd be happy for you right now, if I didn't think you were running."

"I'm not running." Melanie sipped the tea.

"Then you're hiding." Rhoda swooped her hands. "Except this is a much larger closet."

Melanie pushed the tray aside. "I saw Uncle yesterday. I don't feel safe anymore. A part of me hoped he was dead, or long gone. Imagine my surprise when I find out Uncle is none other than Chase's dad. If I'm with Chase there's no avoiding him."

Melanie shook her head in wonder. She was having a hard time seeing the man Chase described as her monster. She rambled. "Chase said his father was a well-respected police officer who was a recovering alcoholic. It was because of Ted giving his life to God that Chase also gave his heart to the Lord."

"Are you sure it was him?" Rhoda asked.

"Yes," Melanie nodded. "It's him. Ted is Uncle. I know it."

"You were only five at the time. Is it possible you could think it's him?"

Melanie glared. "Mom. I wish it weren't him. But, it is."

"That's a heinous crime, I just want you to be sure," Rhoda said.

Melanie bit her lip. A small measure of doubt surfaced. She could be wrong. "I need to ask Janet. She should know."

Rhoda nodded. "I think that's a good idea. Why don't you search online to see if there's a picture of Chase's dad? Janet might not remember his name, but she'll remember his face. By the way, have you spoken to Chase?"

Melanie sniffed. "He's been calling and texting but I have nothing to say to him. I just told him I loved him.

You know how major that was for me to do? Then, this …"

Rhoda tucked her under the chin. "Chase isn't his father. You can't punish him for something he didn't do. He was a kid when all this went down. Do you love him?"

Melanie's heart twisted. The admission flew out of her mouth. "So much it hurts. I love him. I didn't realize how deeply I felt until now. The thought of not seeing him again … it's too much."

"Why are you making Chase pay for his father's crime? Speaking of which, are you going to press charges?"

Melanie shook her head. "I don't know what to do. I'm not making Chase pay but I can't be in Chase's life. Not with that monster around. Plus, how can I put Chase's father in jail? That's if the statute of limitations haven't run out."

Melanie rubbed her temples. A massive headache threatened.

"You should at least speak to Chase," Rhoda said. "That man loves you."

"I think his love would fade if I opened a case against his father. Ted is the only relative Chase has left in this world. No, I can't do that to him." Melanie lowered her head. "But, I can break all ties with Chase. Pretend like I never met him …" Even as she said the words, Melanie knew that would be an impossibility. She would never forget Chase.

Melanie reached for some tissues, but Rhoda had the box in her hand. Gently her mother wiped her face.

Rhoda made Melanie look at her. "Honey, my heart pains for you. You have a lot to think about and I wish I could help you. The only thing I will say is that it's entirely possible Chase is as hurt as you are. Imagine learning his father caused his girlfriend to lose her hearing? Imagine how he must be feeling?"

Melanie knew her eyes showed her misery. "I have thought about that, which is why I was tempted to call and check on him. Chase and his father rebuilt their relationship. I hate knowing I'm the one who could ruin it."

"That's why you should call him," Rhoda urged.

She shook her head. "I think the best thing I can do for Chase now is to leave him alone. I can't make him choose between his family and me."

"That's not your decision to make. It's Chase's."

Melanie changed the subject. "Can you come with me when I go see Janet? Maybe she'll tell me I'm all wrong about Uncle."

Rhoda nodded. "Of course, I'll come. You didn't have to ask." Then she held both hands out. "Gary and I have been praying for you all night through this morning. But now, I want to pray with you. This problem is bigger than us. We have to take it to God."

Melanie took her mother's hands and lowered her head. She would not be able to read Rhoda's lips, but she knew her mother was a prayer warrior. To her surprise, Rhoda squeezed her hands. Melanie opened her eyes to look at her mom.

"Keep your eyes open. I need you to see what I'm saying." Rhoda closed her eyes. "Lord, I come before

You because You're the author of love. No one loves like You do. You've watched out for Melanie all her life. You've been her protector and guide. That's why we're seeking Your face. She has found love. After all these years, she has opened her heart to someone. I prayed and asked You to bring a good man into her life and I know You've answered my prayer. So, I'm depending on You to show Melanie what to do. At this time, Lord, I ask You to expand her heart. Give her more love and a heavy dose of forgiveness. Help her to overcome her scars of the past. Comfort her. Enfold her in Your arms. I pray for Chase as well. Speak to his heart. Cover him under Your wings." Rhoda swallowed.

"Finally, Lord, I pray for Chase's father. Forgive him and … be with him as well." Rhoda began to weep. Melanie's tears blinded her but she kept reading her mother's lips. She could see her mother struggled to say the words. "Help me forgive him. Help Melanie forgive him," Rhoda said. "Send Your healing love to wash away our pain. I pray this prayer in Jesus' name. Amen."

Rhoda opened her eyes. Melanie hugged her mother for a moment. Then she said, "Mom, if I didn't know you were saved, I know it now. Thanks for being an example to me. Thanks for saying the words I couldn't say."

Rhoda nodded. "God will do it. He'll see us through. There's nothing impossible with Him. When the doctors told me I would never have children, God brought you and Tricia into my life. God gave me children. As the song says—I'm paraphrasing here— I'm saying to my soul not to worry. The Lord will make a way, somehow."

***

"Take your sorry butt home," Judd said from behind his desk. "Don't come to work tomorrow with that attitude."

"I don't have an attitude," Chase bit back. It was about 6:30 in the evening and it had been a rough Monday. He and Judd had spent most of the day investigating a murder-suicide. Chase did not understand the phenomenon. It was like it was in style.

"Your attitude's so bad, it's stinking up the place." Judd scooted over to Chase's desk. "What's going on?"

"Nothing's going on. I'm trying to get my paperwork done so I can go home."

"Got a hot date tonight?" Judd fished.

"No. If you must know, Melanie doesn't want to see me anymore."

Judd narrowed his eyes. "Why?"

"I don't want to get into it," Chase mumbled. He pushed his chair to the furthest end away from Judd.

"You might as well tell me because I'm not going to stop until you do."

Chase plopped his hand onto the desk. Might as well. He needed to talk to someone. "Melanie thinks my father is the reason she's deaf." Chase recounted Melanie's horror story.

Judd's eyes widened. "That's crazy. Ted is a

decorated officer of the law. I don't believe it. What did he say when you asked him about it?"

"I didn't ask," Chase said.

"What do you mean you didn't ask?"

"I told my father off. Pretty much told him to hang himself." Chase lowered his eyes with shame. He had never disrespected his father and his cruel choice of words bothered him.

Judd stood and folded his arms. "Let me get this straight. You told a recovering alcoholic who blames himself for your mother and brother's deaths to go hang himself?"

Chase straightened as the implications of Judd's words sunk in. "You don't think he would? I didn't mean it."

Judd strode to his desk and snatched up his keys. "Well I'm not waiting around to find out. I'm going to see Ted." Chase felt the heat of Judd's glare. "Do you think the God you serve would tell you something like that?"

Without waiting for Chase's response, Judd rushed out the door. Imagine God had to use Judd to reprimand him.

"I'm sorry, Lord," Chase whispered. He grabbed his belongings and raced to catch up with Judd. When he burst through the door, Judd was waiting in his car next to Chase's Jeep.

"Knew you'd come to your senses," he said.

Chase jumped into his Jeep. "I'll be right behind you."

"Put on your light bar."

With a nod, Chase complied.

Judd put on his flashing lights and the men sped out of the mall. They arrived at Ted's house in exactly eighteen minutes. Two car doors gave a heavy slam as they jumped out of their vehicles.

"Thank God, his truck is here." Chase crooked his head at the F-150. "Dad!" he called out.

Judd scurried to the back of the house while Chase dashed inside.

"Dad!" he called again, running through the house. He went through every room and bathroom. He even searched the closets. It was empty. Ted was nowhere in sight.

Chase heard a bang on the back door. With his heart hammering in his chest, Chase went to let Judd inside. He craned his neck hoping Ted was behind him.

"He's not out there," Judd said.

"Then where is he?" Chase closed his eyes. "I didn't mean it."

Judd slapped him on the back. "Ted could be out for a walk. We'll wait him out."

Chase made his way into the living area and sat on the couch. Judd sat in the armchair across from him.

"What kind of Christian am I? I could have listened, hear my father's side. But, I was hurt because Melanie couldn't stand the sight of me and I lashed out at him." Chase shook his head.

"Is it that you believe he did it? Is that what's

bothering you?"

"The fear on Melanie's face was real. She is so sure."

"You know until you have no proof or reasonable doubt, Ted is innocent. That's how it works. You can't take the word of a hysterical woman."

Judd's words rang with sense.

"It's in my gut. I saw the look on my father's face. I heard his hesitation. I have a sinking feel in the pit of my stomach that Melanie is right and it's killing me," Chase said. "I tried calling her but she's avoiding me and I can't say I blame her."

Chase's shoulders shook.

"Take some deep breaths and settle down," Judd advised. He picked up the remote and turned on the television to the sports channel.

"What are you doing?" Chase asked.

"We're going to wait here. We'll wait him out. Ted has to come back home sometime. And, when he gets here, we'll ask him. This could all be a mix up," Judd said.

Chase nodded at Judd's hopeful tone.

"In the meantime, why don't you put that faith of yours in action and pray."

Chase arched an eyebrow. "You're advising me to pray."

Judd shrugged. "We have nothing else to do."

"You're right. Thanks, brother, for reminding me. I

do need to seek God's face."

"You're welcome. I know you're not yourself because Melanie has you all twisted. I'm only telling you what you would say to me."

"Mute that," Chase commanded. He dropped to his knees. "Heavenly Father, I've failed You. The minute things get tough for me, I grab onto my old ways. But I thank You for using Judd to speak to me. I'm not that man anymore and I thank You for that. I ask for Your forgiveness for the cruel words I said to my father. Lord, I'm worried about my dad. I don't know where he is and what condition he is in. But, I plead for You to dispatch a special angel to bring my father home. Lord, my dad has come a long way. Please don't let the devil triumph over him. Please remind him of Your love and Your mercy." Chase broke. "I can't lose him, Lord. I've lost too many already. Please bring Dad home. I need to tell him I love him. I pray this prayer, in Jesus' name. Amen."

"Amen," Judd said. "Now we wait."

Chase relaxed his shoulders. "Yes, we'll wait."

Four hours later, Ted staggered into the house. Rip-roaring drunk. Chase sprang to his feet. He could smell the liquor from where he stood.

"I messed up, son. I messed up real bad," Ted said, when he saw Chase standing there.

Chase did not care Ted had compromised his sobriety. Chase did not care he was a monster. All he saw was his father. A father God had returned to him alive and safe. Chase opened his arms.

Ted shook his head. He scrambled to maintain his

stance. "No. I'm drunk. I can barely stand. I'm a sorry mess," Ted wailed. "It's okay if you hate me, forever."

Chase struggled to maintain control. "I don't hate you. God still wants you and so do I."

Chase kept his arms extended and walked over to his father. He did not care that Ted reeked of alcohol. Instead he enfolded his father into his arms. Ted sagged against him.

All Chase could say then was, "Welcome home."

24

"I didn't expect to see you again so soon," Janet said. She coughed into her hand.

"What's the matter with you?" Melanie asked.

"I have this cold that I can't shake." Janet clutched several tissues in her hand. "Never mind me. I'll bounce back soon enough. So, what brings you here?"

"She's here to ask you about Uncle," Rhoda said.

Janet stole a glance at Rhoda. "You look as if you haven't aged. Thanks for taking care of my baby girl."

"It's the favor of God why I look the way I do," Rhoda said. "And, in case you haven't noticed, Melanie's not a baby anymore. We're here because she needs answers. You've got to tell her everything you know about Uncle."

Melanie took Rhoda's hand. "Thanks, Mom," she whispered.

"Uncle was what I called all the men I slept with," Janet said. "I had to tell you something. I didn't want you to think I was loose."

Melanie squinted her eyes. "I remember one Uncle—the one who beat me so hard it deafened me for life. The one who pushed you against the wall and knocked you out while I screamed and yelled for you to help me."

Janet covered her face with her hands. Rhoda tapped the table and Janet resumed eye contact. "I was hoping you didn't remember any of that."

"How could I forget when I'm living with the consequences?" Melanie yelled. She saw a guard step towards them and lowered her voice. "I was there when the cops dragged you away from me. When I woke up, I was deaf. I remember asking the doctor to fix my ears."

"He paid me money." Janet squared her shoulders. "He gave me six hundred dollars not to mention his name."

Six hundred dollars? Her mother had sold her out for a few bucks. Janet reminded Melanie of Esau from the Bible. Esau had sold his birthright to his brother Jacob for a measly bowl of porridge.

Melanie clenched her fists. "What did you do with it? Snort it up your nose? Is that what my life was worth to you?" She cut her eyes at Janet and looked at Rhoda. "Mom, I don't think I can do this."

"We can do all things through Christ," Rhoda said, squeezing her hand.

"Six hundred dollars was a lot of money then." Janet twisted her hands. "Even now. Yes, I used it to get high. Back then, I loved you but I loved the drugs more." She shook her head. "I don't expect you to understand but it's the life of an addict."

"I don't understand," Melanie said.

Janet leaned forward. "Uncle and I were addicts. He was an alcoholic. He was such a good man when he wasn't drinking. He bought you clothes and candy. But once he had a few in him … He was mean. If he were sober, he never would have put a hand on you."

Melanie squinted. "Are you defending him?"

Janet shook her head. "I'm trying to explain. But, you're not giving me a chance."

Rhoda patted Melanie's hand. "Hear her out, honey. Just keep reminding yourself Janet was different then."

Melanie addressed Rhoda. "Mom, I was normal. *Normal.* Don't you get that? I was born with nothing wrong with me but now I'm deaf for the rest of my life." Melanie pointed a finger to Janet. "She sold me out. She caused this."

"I'm surprised to hear you use the word normal," Rhoda said. "Your deafness is your normal. You represent others with disabilities and they would be hurt to hear you say that."

Melanie nodded. "I'm proud of my accomplishments but I didn't know how to put it so Janet would understand."

Janet tapped the table. "I do understand. I've been sorry for twenty-two years. A few months after that night I tried to see you. I stalked the social worker and threatened her because I wanted her to tell me where she had you. I was arrested after that. And while in jail, I tried to kill myself."

Melanie's eyes widened with horror.

"Thank God you didn't succeed," Rhoda spoke and signed.

Melanie nodded. "I—I …"

Janet gave a sad smile. "I'm here. God had plans for me. But back to my story. I confronted Uncle and told him all about what he had done to you. He cried until he vomited all over the floor of my room. Uncle said he didn't remember any of it. He thought I was lying until he heard about it on the news. He was a decorated officer. I was going to turn him in, but he paid me off. He said he had a wife and sons who needed him."

Melanie's heart plummeted. Janet's description sounded like Ted Lawson.

"What is his name?" Melanie asked.

Janet shook her head. "I can't tell you."

"You said he was a police officer. How did you meet him?"

"Cops are the worse adulterers. I met him while he was combing the streets. I might not look like much now but I had body and hips. Lot of men hollered at me."

Melanie shifted. She thought of a cop she loved. "Not all cops are cheats. Some are honest and good men."

"I never met any when I was out there." Janet scoffed. "Why? Is your man a cop?"

Chase was not 'her man' anymore but Melanie saw no need to tell Janet that tidbit. "He's a police officer and he's a man of God."

Janet scoffed. "You know how many preachers I had in my day?"

Melanie glared. "No, and I don't want to know. What I want to know is the name of this police officer."

Janet eased back into her chair. "Why?"

"I need to know." Melanie's lip quivered. "I need to know if he's Chase's father."

Janet's mouth dropped open. "Well if that don't ... I thought nothing could surprise me but ..." She folded her hands. "I doubt it. That would be a big coincidence."

"Or an act of God," Rhoda interjected.

Melanie signed as she spoke. "Why would God do this?"

"We pray all the time and ask God to forgive us as we forgives others. How He does it is entirely up to Him. God allowed all your paths to cross but He has already forgiven each of you. All of you are saved. That in itself is a miracle. Now, God brought you together for you to keep up your end of the bargain."

Melanie narrowed her eyes. "I'm not following you."

Rhoda clapped her hands. "Thank you, Lord for revelation." She leaned further into the table. "Melanie, whether you like it or not, your deafness saved you. If you had stayed with Janet, you could have ended up a junkie or behind bars." Rhoda looked Janet's way. "Sorry."

Janet waved her hand. "It's okay. It's probably true."

Rhonda continued. "Janet had to be locked up because she would never have gotten clean. Now, she's accepted Christ. Ted Lawson, if he is Uncle, is also saved. His guilt eventually led him to Christ. Seeing his father change made Chase give his heart to God. If that isn't a Higher Power at work, I don't know what is."

Trust her mom to inject positivity in her bleak past. Rhoda had taken all the trash, dumped it in a box called salvation, and wrapped it in a pretty bow called forgiveness. Melanie rolled her eyes.

"So now God wants you to pay it forward. He needs you all to forgive each other. That's why you had to fall in love with Chase. Your love for Chase is what made you read Janet's letters. You did it because he felt you should. And, it's your love that will help you forgive Janet and Ted," Rhoda said.

"You missed your calling, Mom," Melanie said. "You should have been a storyteller. That's way too many coincidences."

"It makes sense to me," Janet said.

"God moves in mysterious ways. His ways are not our ways." Rhoda broke out the word from Isaiah.

Melanie leaned into her chair. She pinned Janet with a hard gaze. "Is Ted Lawson Uncle?"

"Get the picture, honey," Rhoda said.

Melanie dug into her pocket and pulled out the picture. She unfolded the paper and held it up for Janet to see. "Is this him?" she asked.

Janet's eyes were so wide Melanie could barely see her irises. She gave a brisk nod. "That's him. That's Uncle." She smiled. "My Teddy Bear."

Melanie collapsed into Rhoda's arms.

25

"Teddy Bear?"

Ted lowered his head. The light blush against his father's cheeks confirmed Chase's fear. "Melanie texted me to ask if you were Teddy Bear aka Uncle." Chase backed up. "I hoped she was wrong but I can see …" He spoke through gritted teeth. "You're Uncle."

"I need to go see her," Ted said, leaning against the stool in Chase's kitchen. "I need to speak to Melanie. Beg for her forgiveness." Ted wrapped Chase's spare robe around him. He lifted a hand to shield his eyes from the Florida sun. Though Chase had closed the blinds, there was no keeping the sun's beam from shining inside.

Chase had taken Ted home with him the night before. Chase did not want Ted staying alone after his relapse. Judd had helped Chase get Ted into his Jeep then followed him home. Once the men settled Ted into the spare bedroom, Judd went home.

Chase had spent a lot of the night in prayer. He was thankful he did not have a shift today so he could devote his energies on Ted.

"Dad, trust me. You're the last person Melanie would want to see." Chase slid the tomato juice in front of him. "Drink this."

Ted rubbed his head. "I forgot how deadly a hangover could be. I'm out of practice, I guess." He took a gulp before wrinkling his nose. "What's in it?"

"Don't worry about it," Chase said. "When you're done, you'll feel better."

"Where did you learn about homemade cures for hangovers?"

"You don't want to know." Chase reached for the croissants he had purchased at *Dunkin Donuts* the day before. "I wasn't always saved. You know that." He opened the refrigerator for the butter. He offered it to Ted. Chase returned to the refrigerator. He gathered a stalk of kale, a lime, a green apple, and a cucumber to make a smoothie. He retrieved a glass out of his dishwasher and placed it on the counter.

Ted took small sips of his tomato juice. "Thank you, son."

Chase gave a brisk nod and worked on washing and chopping his ingredients. He was not in the mood for conversation. Chase poured all the contents from the bowl into the blender. The thought that his father committed such a heinous crime was tough news.

"That's green." Ted was trying hard to make conversation.

"It's good."

Chase poured his concoction into a long glass and slipped onto the stool next to his father. Chase avoided eye contact. "Dad, I need you to tell me everything."

"I don't remember," Ted said. "But, I'll do my best

to fill in the blanks. I was drunk for most of my life. I held it together on the job but as soon as my shift ended … one night I was cruising down Easy Street and I saw a woman strutting in four-inch heels in this tight mini skirt. I stopped …"

Chase swallowed a huge portion of his drink. For a moment, he entertained the thought of adding something stronger. Then he rebuked the thought. Chase prayed for strength instead.

"I rolled down my window and asked her name and if she needed a ride. It was so late. I had good intentions. I meant to take her home but once she was inside my car, Janet made a pass at me. I was weak and before I knew five months had gone by."

"Five months?" Chase's chest heaved. "You cheated on Mom that whole time?"

Ted touched Chase's arm. "I was young and stupid."

Chase snarled. "Don't give me young and stupid, Dad. That's a copout. Was Janet the only one?"

Ted shifted his gaze. "There were women here and there. Nothing serious. There was something about Janet, though. She was … different."

"Janet was an addict." Chase rose off the stool. He drank the rest of his smoothie to keep from spewing the terrible words the enemy brought to his mind. Chase was not going to dishonor his God or his father.

"Yes, and Janet is my past."

Chase glared. "What about Melanie? How do you explain what you did to her?" He drew deep, long breaths. "I told you someone beat Melanie until she lost her hearing and you said nothing. In fact, you said the person who did that deserved to be hung."

"I did," Ted said. He stood and walked over to Chase. "I didn't remember what I had done when we were talking. It was over twenty years ago. I wasn't even thinking about that."

"Melanie thinks about it. Every day of her life," Chase said. "Every morning she wakes up she's reminded she used to hear. Melanie's a dancer. A really good dancer who cannot hear the music." Chase splayed his hands. "Don't you get that?"

Ted wiped his forehead. "I was drunk. I don't remember hurting her. If Janet hadn't confronted me I wouldn't have known."

"That's nonsense and I'm not buying it." Chase folded his arms. "Your fists had to have been bruised or something."

Ted rubbed his palms. "My hands were sore and bruised. I couldn't recall how I hurt them. Then Janet told me what I had done and of course it was all over the news."

Chase narrowed his eyes. "Why didn't Janet turn you in? I know she was high but I can't believe a mother wouldn't want to see the man who hurt her child punished."

Ted shifted his gaze. "I paid her off."

"You what?" Chase shook his head. Just when he thought it could not get any worse. "Who are you?"

Ted jutted his jaw. "I'm me. The father you've

known the past three years. God changed me and I'm holding onto that. But years ago I did a horrible thing and I'm filled with regret. But God has forgiven me. All my past is under the blood."

Chase bit back the snarky comment. "Jesus might have paid it all but you still have consequences."

Ted squinted. "Are you going to turn me in?"

"You should turn yourself in."

"You don't think I've thought about it?" Ted asked. "But then I say, what's the point?"

"The point is it's the right thing to do."

Ted quit fighting. "I'm scared. So many people looked up to me. I'm scared to see their disappointed faces and knowing my actions put it there."

"I'm scared to look Melanie in the face knowing your actions damaged her for a lifetime."

Ted dragged himself from the kitchen to the bedroom. To Chase, Ted appeared broken and his heart constricted. He thought of Melanie and his chest tightened. He felt pulled in opposite directions. Chase blew out a huge expanse of air. He loved them both but he could not have them both. The question was, should he go with the man who gave him life or the woman who was his life?

Chase rubbed his temples. He closed his eyes. "What do I do, Lord?"

The Lord was quiet.

He needed to do something. He pulled on his fingers. He ran his fingers through his hair. He wandered the kitchen.

Then inspiration struck. Chase rushed into his bedroom to get his phone. He pulled up the pictures of Melanie dancing.

Chase flipped through the pictures. His heart smiled seeing Melanie's poses. She soared as high as an eagle. Her swanlike grace was evident by her extended arm and pointed toes. He cupped the phone in his palm and walked out to the patio.

Chase squatted on his workbench. He ripped off the blanket he had used to preserve the wood. Chase ran his hand along the edges of the Basswood. Then he picked up his whittling tools.

26

"The only person sulking should be me," Tricia said. She bit into a pineapple chunk. "I'm bigger than a whale. I'm about to charge admission for a view."

Melanie eyed Tricia's rounded stomach. Tricia was five months along but she was huge. Her obstetrician said there was no need for concern, though. Nevertheless, Tricia tried to control her urgings with salads and fruit.

"You're beautiful and I'm not sulking," Melanie signed.

Tricia adjusted her body on the green oversized loveseat, then plopped her feet on the ottoman. Emory purchased the sofa because after two months of camping out in her room, Tricia screamed for a change of scenery.

Melanie had spent the night. She had visited with Rachel and stopped by Tricia's house to update her. Rachel's trial would begin in two weeks. Both Melanie and Tricia had prayed for their friend but they knew Rachel would do time. The question was, for how long.

Melanie stretched as her aching back protested bunking on Tricia's couch. She missed her deep sleep number bed mattress.

"Why don't you give Chase a call?" Tricia asked.

Melanie shook her head. "Too much time has passed. He's most likely moved on by now. Men like him don't stay single for long."

"Didn't you say Chase hadn't dated for three years?"

Melanie nodded.

"I find it hard to believe he's found someone new, or even looking," Tricia said. She saw Tricia cover her mouth. "Excuse me. I burped."

Melanie shrugged. "I couldn't tell." She swung her feet to the floor. "I'm trying to stop thinking about Chase. There's no hope for us."

Tricia's eyes softened with compassion. "There's always hope. Love brings hope."

"His father beat me."

"Chase is not his father."

"He chose Ted."

"He shouldn't have to choose."

"I'm not having anything to do with Uncle," Melanie said. "If I'm with Chase, I'd have to deal with him."

"You don't have to deal with Uncle. Uncle is gone. You said yourself he's changed. You'd be dealing with Ted."

Melanie pursed her lips. "They are one and the same," she signed.

"Can you get me some strawberries?"

Melanie grinned. "You're like a garbage disposal."

Tricia threw a pillow her way. Melanie jumped to her feet and went into the kitchen. She washed and chopped two cups of strawberries, one for herself and one for Tricia. She returned into the living area.

"Here you go." Melanie handed Tricia the fruit.

Tricia ate several pieces. Melanie bit into a strawberry but her stomach was closed for business. She put her fruit cup on the coffee table. She had lost about ten pounds. Melanie knew it was because her appetite had waned and she had been dancing twice a day for hours. Dancing was meant to distract her heart from Chase but it had the opposite effect. The more she danced, the more Chase flooded her mind.

Not dancing was not a cure. She had avoided the studio for a week. But, somehow, some way Chase invaded her thoughts. She saw Tricia's waving her hand in her peripheral vision. Melanie faced her.

"What's that face about?" Tricia asked. She held up a hand. "Don't tell me. You're thinking about Chase."

"I can't shake him," Melanie said.

"Maybe you're not supposed to."

Melanie gave Tricia the evil eye. "Obviously, you've not been listening to a word I've been saying."

"Have you tried praying?"

Melanie lifted her hands. "I've prayed and prayed and I've prayed some more. I find myself praying for Chase, asking God to keep him safe on the road."

"Girl, I don't know what else to say. You've got it

bad."

"Tell me about it. What was my life like before Chase Lawson?" Melanie mumbled. Her feet tingled. "I'm going to the studio."

"You're there so much, why don't you buy the place?" Tricia threw her head back and laughed.

Melanie kissed Tricia on the forehead. "I'm going home to shower and change. Do you need anything else before I leave?"

"Hand me the remote. I'm hooked on the Maury show."

Melanie wrinkled her nose. "How can you watch that?"

"I was channel surfing one day and now I'm hooked."

Melanie took in Tricia's sparkling eyes. "I'm glad you know your baby's daddy."

"I am, too." Tricia's eyes warmed. "God has been good to us, sis. Look where we were, where we could have been, and where God brought us."

Melanie nodded. "Every day, I thank God for the Benson's. I wouldn't trade them for the world."

Tricia's eyes pleaded. "That's probably how Chase feels about his father. Ted is all the family he has left. Surely, love can cover the hideous past. I'll be praying for you."

Melanie swallowed. Tricia's words hit Melanie's heart. She gave Tricia a hug before making her way out of the residence. Melanie trudged toward her vehicle.

Once she was inside, she gripped the wheel. "Lord, help me know what to do."

My grace is sufficient, flowed into her spirit.

Melanie mulled on that as she drove home. Twenty minutes later she was on her way to the studio. She pulled into the vacant lot and parked into one of the spaces. Melanie scrunched her nose and looked at her watch. It was close to noon. "Where's everyone?" she voiced aloud.

Melanie walked up to the door. There was a blue paper taped to it. She squinted her eyes and read the fine-print. The studio was closed. Her stomach dropped. Eviction notices from the sheriff's office were on the door. There was a scribbled note of apology from Delia and Hank.

Melanie noticed there were several notes taped to the door. She slid her eyes back to the notice and shook her head. But this made no sense. She was here a week ago. The Hartman's had smiled at her like they had no cares or concerns. Not once had they mentioned their money troubles. Melanie read the notice again.

Tricia's words teased her ears. *You're there so much, why don't you buy the place?* Melanie stood still. God had spoken. She knew it as clear as she knew her own name. Melanie missed working but knew she would never number crunch ever again. But dancing, she could do every minute and every hour.

Melanie plucked a few of the notes off the door and read them. Many of the parents had left their phone numbers. They expressed sadness at the studio's closing. Melanie felt like God had left these notes for her to read. She snatched the other notes and quickly scanned them.

Clutching the papers in her hand, Melanie zoomed toward her car. She tossed the papers on her car seat and grabbed her cell phone. Melanie raced over to the door and snapped a picture of the notice. There was a courthouse auction scheduled and a number to call.

Melanie's heart raced. She rushed back to Tricia's home with the papers in her hand. "Tricia!" she yelled, bounding inside Tricia's home.

Tricia jerked awake and grabbed her stomach. "You're loud enough to wake me if I were six feet under."

"Sorry if I scared you but I'm just so excited," Melanie said in a much lower tone. She scurried over to her sister and practically shoved the papers into Tricia's hands. "You've got to read this."

Tricia eyes widened. "Wow. God is moving on your behalf." She waved the papers. "You can't let the studio go."

Melanie's head bobbed. "I need you to call the number for me and get me the information."

Tricia grabbed her cell phone. Melanie flew into the kitchen and pulled out the miscellaneous drawer. Tricia kept her appliance warranties, batteries—pretty much anything—in that drawer. Melanie rummaged in the drawer for a pen and paper.

Tricia eyes flashed with excitement. She was talking fast but kept moving her head so Melanie had a hard time deciphering all that was being said.

Melanie plopped next to Tricia and tapped her feet.

"What's going on?" she asked.

Tricia wagged her forefinger for Melanie to hand her the paper. With a flourish, Tricia wrote down a date and time. April 27. Next Tricia wrote 9:15 a.m. Finally, she wrote down a figure and Melanie's eyes popped wide.

Melanie cupped her mouth. The Guys and Dolls studio was on the market for an unbelievable price. Melanie laughed when she saw the paltry sum. Who could this be but God?

"Lord, why do You love me so?" she shouted.

Tricia ended the call and opened her hands wide. Melanie went into Tricia's arms. They hugged and giggled.

Tricia broke the embrace first. "Get to the bank and secure that cashier's check. Then call a real estate attorney to handle the paperwork."

Melanie did a high kick. "I'm going to own the Guys and Dolls! I can't wait to tell Mom and Dad. Mom will probably tell me it's about time."

"Yes, she will." Tricia grinned. "April 27th can't come fast enough!"

Melanie froze. "April 27th. That's Rachel's court date," she whispered.

Tricia tapped her nose. "Are you sure?"

With a hollow stomach, Melanie sunk into the couch. She signed the words as the breath had left her body. "Yes, I'm sure. Same date. Same time."

"You need to go. This is the opportunity of a

lifetime," Tricia signed.

"When I saw Rachel, she was broken. She's scared to face the jury. I promised her I'd be there."

"I can go," Tricia said.

Melanie shook her head. "You can't put your baby in danger. Your health is important."

"So is your dream."

The Guys and Dolls studio flashed before her mind. Melanie could already see the eager young girls' faces as she greeted them for class. Suddenly, she had never wanted something so much in her life.

Tricia waved a hand. "Your attorney can go in your place."

"No, I have to be there. I need to," Melanie said. "I'll speak with Rachel. I'm sure she'll understand."

27

"Don't bother coming," Rachel said.

"It's only one day. I've been by your side. I need to buy that studio."

Rachel pursed her lips. "While I'm in here rotting away, you're dancing. I need to have one friend in that courtroom. I understand why Tricia can't be here but to get tossed aside for a block of wood is reprehensible."

"Rachel, you're not being fair. I didn't set the date. I promise you, I'll head here as soon as I'm done."

Rachel folded her arms. "If you don't come April 27th, then don't come back."

"How can you be so selfish? Were you always this selfish and I just didn't see it?" Melanie knew she was yelling and drew a breath to hold her temper in check. "I've been here to see you twice a week. I've paid your attorney fees and put money in your commissary. Now this is one thing I must do for me." She jabbed a finger into her chest. "I need to do this."

Rachel glared. "Then go ahead. Do you. I'll do me." She jumped to her feet and gestured to the guard.

"Rachel, please …"

"I'm done," Rachel signed. Without a backward

glance, she returned to her cell.

Melanie looked around the room. An elderly lady smiled at her. Her eyes held sympathy. Melanie knew her cheeks were on fire. With as much dignity as she could muster, Melanie exited the visiting room.

Hurt pierced her chest and tears flowed down her cheeks. After all their years of friendship, Rachel was all about Rachel. Melanie reasoned that Rachel was in the fight of her life. Then Melanie shook her head. Rachel knew what dancing meant to her. She should have at least understood.

Melanie pulled into her driveway but did not want to be alone. She walked around to her parent's entrance and used her key to enter.

Wandering through the house, Melanie called out. "Mom! Dad!" She headed to the patio and poked her head outside.

Gary was sitting in the lounge chair. He looked her way. "Hey, honey. Your mother's at Publix."

Melanie's chin wobbled. She headed straight into her father's arms. Melanie breathed in his Old Spice scent as Gary patted her on the back. Melanie released her pain in gut-wrenching sobs.

Several minutes later, she pulled away. "I'm sorry, Dad. I think I've lost Rachel as a friend."

Gary furrowed his brows. "What you mean?"

"I told her about the auction. It's the same date and time as her court date. Rachel's furious because she thinks I'm turning my back on her."

"Baby Girl, Rachel has turned her back on God.

Don't think for a minute God wasn't telling her not to get involved with a married man. She made the choice to hold a child for ransom. She could've called the police but Rachel saw dollar signs. Don't feel guilty about doing something for yourself."

"I still feel bad," Melanie said.

"That's because you care so much for others. Everything you do, you do with someone else in mind. It's okay to think of yourself," Gary said. He touched Melanie's cheek. "Rhoda and I rejoice that you're finally seeing yourself as worthy. Melanie, your wants and needs are important and it's time you realized that."

Melanie lowered her eyes. How could her father know her so well? Gary's hand grazed her chin.

"You suffered so much trauma as a little girl. Rhoda and I wondered if you would ever recover. We prayed for you every day. We did our best and we're so proud of all your accomplishments."

Melanie sniffed back tears. "You and Mom saved me."

Gary shook his head. "No. God did that. If anything, you helped increased our faith." He laughed. "Rhoda and I didn't know about praying until God blessed us with daughters."

Melanie smiled.

"No matter how much love we gave you, we felt you held back. It was like you were afraid to love. It was like you felt you didn't deserve it."

Melanie's eyes widened. "How did you know?"

"It's the parent's job to make their child feel secure.

Your mother put you out of her bed and made you sleep in a closet. That has deep rooted effects which play out in ways you can't even imagine." He held her arms. "But, I want you to know you're worthy. Worthy enough that God closed Rhoda's womb because He knew you would need us. Your counselor was the one who made us put you into dance."

"I didn't know that. You never told me."

Gary nodded. "Yes, she did. Melanie, you may not remember this but your first two weeks home, you didn't say a word. All you did was follow us around with sad eyes. You didn't leave Rhoda's side and you had nightmares. Some nights we had you in our bed and others Rhoda slept with you in your room. Your room had everything a little girl could want but you were scared to sleep in your bed. Rhoda cried every night. That's when the counselor suggested dancing. Dancing would give you a way to express your feelings since you didn't have the words."

"How come I can't recall any of that?" All Melanie remembered was a happy childhood filled with love and dance.

"Coping mechanism." Gary smiled and put a hand on his chin. "I'll never forget your first class. You executed a plié and your arm swooped in the air. I felt chills. I knew you had found your thing. That night you slept in your bed alone with no nightmares."

Melanie gulped. What a testimony. "Thanks for telling me," she whispered.

"Dancing is in your bones. When Christ returns, I'm sure you'll be in the praise dancing section. I get a glimpse of heaven when I see you perform." Gary wiped his eyes. "That's why it hurts that you gave up Juilliard because of me. I knew how much it cost you…"

Melanie hugged her father tight. "It was a price I paid willingly. I love you. I have no regrets. If I had to, I'd do it again."

She excused herself to use the restroom and wash her face. Melanie had never seen Gary so emotional. She grabbed the tissues from the end table in the living room on her way back to the patio.

When she returned, Gary was more composed. He pulled several tissues from the box, dabbed at his eyes, and blew his nose.

"Get that studio," he said. "Not just for you but for me."

"Thanks, Dad," Melanie said.

Gary rubbed his chin. "You said something I want you to think about. You said you loved me so much you willingly sacrificed your career. Do you love Chase that much? Is he worth the sacrifice that comes with forgiveness?"

She tilted her head. "What do you mean?"

"Is your love for Chase greater than the pain his father caused?"

Melanie narrowed her eyes. "If I remember right, Mom and I had to beg you not to go after Ted Lawson. You wanted me to press charges. In fact, I've never seen you lose it like you did when we came back from the prison. Now you're telling me I need to forgive him."

Gary nodded. "I've had three months to calm down. I've been watching you and your eyes are sad again. You've lost weight and you're not sleeping but you're grown so I kept my mouth shut and prayed. Ted Lawson ripped your security blanket and all your past hurt resurfaced. That's why you've been dancing so much. Even at church, you've been going through the motion."

Goodness. Her father was very observant. He had read her right, too. "I didn't know you were seeing all that. Most of the time your eyes are glued to the TV screen."

"Pretense."

Melanie chuckled.

"Anyway, once I saw what being without Chase was like for you, I've been praying for God to heal your heart. You told me Ted's saved. Melanie, this is going to sound strange but God turned your sorrow into joy. He won the war using His own weapon. Salvation. God has slain your monster. It took me a minute to see it, but God showed me that. He works in mysterious ways and His ways are past finding out. It's the only thing that eased my anger."

Melanie straightened. God had slain her monster. He did it His way, without bloodshed. That revelation gave her goose bumps. "You gave me a lot to think about. Thanks, Dad."

"Pray and fast. It'll help you."

Melanie left Gary on the patio and went into her apartment. She sat on her bed. God had opened her eyes. Melanie's past flashed before her. She saw Him there each step of the way. God was there with her through all her trials.

Melanie experienced a great sense of awe. She could not understand that kind of love. A verse from Romans 8 teased her senses. "And we know that all things work together for good to them that love God, to them who are called according to His purpose."

Melanie received the word. All things worked for her good. She looked heavenwards and asked, "God, do you love me that much?"

Yes, I do.

28

"Nadine's pregnant," Judd said.

Chase stomped on the brake. He and Judd were in his Jeep driving down US 41 when Judd broke the news. They were on their way to Best Buy to purchase Ted a new television. Ted's older floor model gave out the night before.

Judd's body jerked forward. A car honked at Chase. Chase lifted a hand to say, "Sorry." He could see the driver behind him flailing his hand and changed lanes.

Chase turned into the Chick-fil-A and parked. "Don't drop news on me like that when I'm driving."

"I'm sorry," Judd said.

"How long have you known?"

"Since that night Nadine called."

Chase's eyes bulged. "That was three months ago and you're just now telling me?"

"I ... I needed time to process. I'm going to be a father. It took me three months to come to terms with that."

Chase leaned forward. "You needed three months to accept your child?"

"No, it took me all this time before Nadine would bring herself to speak to me. She's slammed the door in my face twice and hung up on me more times than I can count," Judd said. "When Nadine told me about the baby, I asked if she were sure I was the father. I mean I wore a condom and all …"

Chase laughed. "Please tell me you didn't say that to a classy woman like Nadine. You're experienced enough to know nothing but abstinence is foolproof."

Judd lowered his eyes. "Those words flew out of my mouth before my common sense kicked in." He chuckled. "You should have seen Nadine's reaction. Her anger was a sight to behold. As big as I am, I don't know how she did it but Nadine threw me out of her house. My butt literally hit the curb. I was too ashamed to tell you."

"You're my best friend, Judd. Of course I'd stand by you." Chase opened his car door. "Let's grab something to eat since we're here."

"I'm not that hungry. I'll get a lemonade." Judd opened his passenger door.

They walked in step toward the entrance. Chase said, "I thought you and Nadine were in love. The timing might be off, but a baby's still good news. Any child is a blessing from God."

"Children are also a million dollar investment. I'm in love with Nadine. I've never felt that way about a woman before. But, I wasn't ready to have another child. Look how things worked out with my last baby mama. I promised myself any other children I brought into the world would be when I'm married."

Chase opened the door to the restaurant. He and Judd stepped aside so a young mother and her toddler could exit. "That could still happen."

As usual the place was packed with the lunchtime crowd. There was a ball pit for the toddlers to play in on his left. Chase scanned the rest of the place. There were two booths and two tables available. Since there was only one person ahead of them, Chase did not worry about seating.

Judd rubbed his chin. "I couldn't agree with you more. Nadine's divorce has been finalized for about six weeks but she won't marry me."

Chase's nose welcomed the smell of fried chicken. He stepped up to the counter and ordered the deluxe chicken sandwich combo with lemonade. Then he glanced at Judd. "What you want?" He tapped his feet to the gospel music playing in the background.

"I'll get my own but thanks," Judd said.

With a nod, Chase paid for his meal. To his surprise, Judd ordered two of the 12-count nugget meals.

"I thought you weren't hungry," he said once Judd returned to his side. They stood waiting on their orders.

"Yes but I'm eating for two now," Judd joked.

Chase poked him in the ribs good-naturedly. "Keep eating like that and your stomach will show it."

"Nope. That's why I work out. So I can eat what I want."

Their orders came up. Both men held their trays and walked to the condiment stand. Judd grabbed barbecue sauce for his nuggets while Chase snagged two ketchup packets and mustard. By mutual consent they headed to the booth in the back of the room. They settled into the seat and blessed their meal.

"Why won't Nadine marry you?" Chase asked, spreading the mustard on his chicken sandwich.

Judd used his fork to capture his nugget then dunked it in barbecue sauce. "I think her parents are influencing her. They weren't too thrilled about our, uh, affair."

Chase took a bite of his chicken sandwich. "She doesn't seem like the type whose parents could push her around."

Judd nodded. "If I hadn't acted like an a— an idiot, she would be with me. But as you warned me, she was vulnerable. She hasn't said it in so many words but I think Nadine thinks I'm only asking her because it's the right thing to do. I don't think she believes I'm in love with her."

"Then you have to make her believe," Chase said. "You can't let her slip through your fingers."

Judd stared. "Same goes for you. Why haven't you reached out to Melanie?" He sipped on his lemonade. "This should have been tea," he said, referencing the current trend on the Internet with Kermit the frog. Kermit sipped tea while spilling the plain truth.

Chase shook his head. "Me and Melanie's situation is way different than yours and Nadine. We loved each other but asking Melanie to overlook what my father did would be way too much." He jutted a chin toward Judd. "You and Nadine both have pride standing in your way. You can boot that out with one swing of your leg. Mine takes a bulldozer."

"Or some good old-fashioned fasting and praying," Judd said. He took another sip of his lemonade and stared.

"I have been praying," Chase said.

"And fasting?" Judd asked.

Chase sipped his lemonade. Judd cracked up.

"You're a church man. You know about that better than me. My mother fasted and prayed for me and look how good I turned out."

Chase chuckled then confessed what was in his heart. "I miss Melanie. Every day I think of her. I've picked up my phone countless times to call but changed my mind. What can I say to make her feel better?"

Judd shook his head. "There's nothing you can do to make Melanie feel better. But you can love her. Love her so much that it covers all the bad of her past."

Chase's heart leapt. "I can do that." He tilted his head. "Come with me to church this Saturday."

"What time should I be there?"

Chase had opened his mouth to lecture Judd on why he should be in church when Judd's words sunk in. "You're coming?"

Judd nodded. "I'm trying everything else and it's not working. I need to be in church plus some prayer and fasting."

Chase shifted. "Tell you what. Let's go all in and do a sit-in. You, me, and my dad at my place. Friday night.

Come around nine. The three of us will demolish the devil's plans. Love will conquer all."

Judd laughed. "You sound like a Disney character."

Chase covered his embarrassment by eating his fries. He knew his face was all shades of red but for the first time in weeks, he had hope.

They finished their meals and tossed their trays.

"Thanks for coming to Chick-fil-A'," one of the workers said.

Chase and Judd waved and left the restaurant.

"I feel at home every time I go in there," Judd said. "They have the cheeriest staff on the planet."

Chase nodded. "I feel it too."

They zigzagged through the pick-up-line and Chase clicked the unlock button to deactivate the alarm. The men got in and Chase started up the Jeep. As he backed out he said, "I've been whittling."

Judd slapped his arm. "What? When? We've been working some serious cases of late. When do you find the time?"

"I haven't been sleeping well," Chase admitted. "I've been making dancers. Well, *one* dancer in particular."

"That's great. You haven't whittled since your mother and brother died. Chase, that's awesome."

"I used pictures I had of Melanie dancing as inspiration." Chase cleared his throat. "I'd love for you to see them. Get your thoughts."

"I'd be honored, friend. How many did you make?" Judd asked.

"I made six of them. I hope to give them to Melanie as an engagement present."

"Engagement ..." Judd trailed off.

Chase stole a glance his way. Judd had a wide smile on his face. Chase refocused on the road. "Before talking to you, I wasn't sure what I would do. But I'm putting God on the job."

"You should wrapped them up real nice and put the ring on the dancer's hand."

"What a good idea," Chase said. "Don't tell me you're a romantic."

"Don't tell anyone. If you have any ideas for Nadine and myself, swing it by me."

"I do know what you have to do," Chase said, turning into the Best Buy.

"Then why you making me fast and pray and all that. What do I have to do?"

"Grovel."

Judd scoffed.

Chase executed a smart turn into a small spot. "Trust me. It works."

"How am I going to look groveling at her feet? I can't go out like that."

"Grovel," Chase said again, with much more force.

"All right. I hear you." Judd groaned. In a conspiratorial tone, he said, "If you tell anyone ..."

Chase shook his head. "I wouldn't."

Judd shoved him. Chase held his arm. "What did you do that for? Groveling doesn't make you less of a man. So ease off on the testosterone."

"All right. Nadine's got to marry me. I definitely don't want two baby mamas. I need a wife."

"She's the one," Chase said. "Do what you have to do. I know what's better than groveling. If her son fell in love with you …"

Judd rubbed his hands together. "I love Steven already, so that's easy."

"That's the way to Nadine's heart. Give her son a real man to look up to. Pursue Steven. Nadine will follow." Chase patted Judd on the back. "Now, let's bring my father into the present with a high-def television."

29

Melanie held her orange and brown faux fur blanket in her hands. If she was to spend another night with Tricia on that couch, she was coming prepared. She used her spare key to enter Tricia's home.

Tricia was laid out on her chair watching the *Real Housewives of Atlanta.*

"You're killing brain cells," Melanie signed as she wiped her feet on the large welcome mat.

Tricia turned on the subtitles. Melanie held up her Bible. "We have a date with God, remember?"

Tricia clicked the OFF button.

"Where's Emory?" Melanie asked. He was supposed to join them.

"He's been called in to work so he's happy you'll be here. Ever since I've been on bed rest, he's been packing up his overtime hours. He plans on taking Family Medical Leave once this little guy arrives."

"Little guy?" Melanie smiled.

"I think so," Tricia said. "Just have a feeling."

"I intend to spoil him or her big time," Melanie said.

"I'm counting on it, Auntie Melanie." Tricia pointed at the rose pink Bible on the couch. "Can you reach that for me? Let's get our minds in the place for prayer."

"Thanks for praying with me, sis," Melanie said, handing Tricia the Bible. She had called Tricia and set up the Friday night prayer vigil. Her sister had readily agreed. Melanie had been on fasting all day.

"No worries. I'm sorry I couldn't be on fasting with you. Remember when The Tres Amigas went on all night-prayer-fest when Emory proposed. I'm returning the favor."

Melanie nodded. "I miss Rachel," she signed.

Tricia's eyes saddened. "We'll pray for her but Rachel's on a different track. Maybe God needs her behind bars so she can find Him again."

"I hope so," Melanie said.

Melanie and Tricia leaned into each other for support. Melanie remembered Rachel's parting words. Her chest heaved with pain.

Tricia read her mind. "God's got Rachel. We'll leave her in God's hands and then as far as I'm concerned it's handled. Let's focus on why we're here."

Melanie nodded. "The other night God spoke through Dad. He told me God has slain my monster. I don't have anything to fear when it comes to Unc—I mean, Ted, ever again."

Tricia nodded. "But there's a wedge there."

Melanie touched her chest. "Yes. A wedge of pain mixed with anger."

Tricia flipped through her Bible pages. "Let's read Romans 8."

Goose bumps rose on Melanie's flesh. "God gave me a word from that very chapter."

"Good. So we know He's leading." Tricia recited the words.

Melanie whispered along with her. When Tricia was finished, they joined hands. They sang songs and read Psalms for the next hour. Melanie felt God's presence. She knew angel's surrounded them. They prayed for Rachel. They prayed about the dance studio.

"I'll pray for you, now," Tricia said. As usual Melanie kept her eyes open so she could 'touch and agree' when necessary.

"Lord, we come before Your presence because You're a deliverer. You've brought Melanie this far. You've made her prosper and rise above her childhood. Now, Lord, we come before You asking You to complete the healing in Melanie's life. She knows You've already fought her battle and won. She knows she has nothing to fear in Ted Lawson but God the enemy has crippled her with fear. Right now, as a child of God with all the authority You've given me, I bind all the pain and fear of the past. I bind it in the name of Jesus."

"Hallelujah," Melanie said. "Yes, Lord."

"You said whatever I bind on earth is bound in heaven, and I'm standing on Your word. I ask God that as You've forgiven Ted and thrown his past sins in the sea of forgetfulness, You will help Melanie to do the same."

Melanie gulped. Tears streamed down her face. "Help me, Lord," she whispered.

"Help her realize she's standing on top of her past and her future is above. Help her look up unto the hills. Help her press toward a higher calling and forget everything that is behind. Right now, in Your name, Jesus ..." Tricia broke off and began to speak in a heavenly language.

Melanie lifted her hands. "Help me, Jesus."

"Pour it out," Tricia said. "Forget about me being here and talk to God."

Melanie nodded and lifted her hands. The women shouted praises and paid homage to God. Just before daybreak, Melanie prayed. The words burst out of her mouth.

"Lord, I thank You for the man You've sent into my life. I love Chase with all my heart. Just as I was able to admit that, I find out his father was the reason I'm deaf." She doubled over. "For years I wondered who Uncle was. Then when I saw his face ... Jesus help me," she wailed, "Everything came flooding back. I know Ted Lawson is a changed man. I know he's been made new but there's no going back for me. There's no do-over. I'll be deaf for the rest of my life. Never hearing again ... I've never heard Chase's voice. I'll never hear my children ..."

Melanie sobbed. Her shoulders shook unable to carry the burden of her pain.

You can hear me.

Melanie straightened. "Yes, Lord. I can hear you," she said.

Give me all.

She wiped her face and looked at Tricia.

Tricia held her arms open. "Release it. God wants you to let it go once and for all so you can move on." She opened her Bible. "I'm going to paraphrase Revelations 21 verse 4 for you. God shall wipe away all tears from your eyes. There will be no more sorrow, nor crying, neither shall there be any more pain: for the former things are passed away."

Melanie fell to her knees. Her curls framed her face and her body was wet from sweat. She lay on the floor and cried to God, knowing His Spirit would make intercession for her.

"At this I put Ted Lawson before you. I ask God that You will help him get over any guilt he's holding as well. Help us both move forward." Melanie sat up with a start. Her eyes were wide. Had those words left her mouth?

Her eyes connected with Tricia. Tricia face was red and swollen. "Won't God do it?" she said.

Melanie rolled her eyes and said, "You've been watching too much reality TV." She looked through the blinds and saw the sun peeking through. "Thanks, Tricia, for tarrying with me all night."

Tricia waved her hand. "It was a pleasure. I slept through the day and my spirit was thirsty for a night with God. Now help me up. I've got to use the bathroom."

Melanie helped her sister stand. "After all that praying we did, you'll have one blessed baby."

"You know it," Tricia said. "And, you'll have a blessed husband."

***

"I know God is here," Chase said. The men were gathered on Chase's patio. It was enclosed and insulated so they were cool. Chase had played Chris Tomlin, Mandisa, and Tasha Cobb. But it was Nicole Miller's voice that ushered God's presence inside the place.

Ted tilted his head upwards. "Lord, I worship You. You are worthy to be praised. I thank You for Your blood which washed away all my sins."

Chase worshiped with his father before looking over in Judd's direction.

Judd's body hung off the lounge chair. His head bobbed as he struggled to stay awake.

"Judd," Chase whispered. He went over and shook his friend awake.

Judd wobbled to his feet.

"It's right before dawn. Time for you to pray."

Judd yawned. "I've prayed so much tonight, I've made up for my teenage and college years. I'm hungry."

Chase stifled a grin at Judd's mumbled words. "Get serious. God is here so make your request known." He crooked his head to where Ted stood praising.

"Why didn't you say so?" Judd's facial expression

changed. He lowered his head. Chase closed his eyes and touched Judd's shoulder.

Judd began. "Lord, I've been avoiding You for most of my life. I'm making a mess of everything without You. I've decided it's time I put myself in Your hands. Amen."

Chase's eyes popped open. "Hallelujah!" he shouted.

Judd lifted his head.

"Did I hear you right?" Chase asked.

Judd nodded. "I'm ready. I need God in my life."

Chase ran for his Bible and found I John 1. He read verse 4. "If we confess ours sins, He is faithful and just to forgive us our sins, and to cleanse us from all unrighteousness."

Judd's eyes widened. "You mean I've got to tell God all the bad things I've done. We could be here for days."

Chase chuckled. Ted must have finished his praying because he came and joined them.

"You can sum it up by confessing you're a lifetime sinner and you're sorry," Ted said.

Judd nodded and closed his eyes. "God, I'm sorry for all my wrongs. I'll be a sinner in this lifetime and the next if you don't save me."

Chase's body shook with laughter. "In Jesus' name. Amen."

"Amen. So let it be," Ted said.

Chase held up his hands. "Heavenly Father, I approach you on Melanie's behalf. Like Isaac with Rebecca, I loved her at her first sight. I know she's the one for me. I ask You to clear the path for the both of us. Help us find our way back to each other. I pray this prayer, in Jesus' name. Amen."

When the sun rose, the men praised God. Judd clapped his hands and danced in the Spirit. Chase watched his friend and marveled. He planned to dance as well, with Melanie by his side. And, he would.

Chase prayed a final prayer of thanksgiving. When he opened his eyes, his father was gone.

30

Melanie pulled into her driveway a little after 10 a.m. that Saturday morning. There was a black F-150 in the space where her mother's minivan was usually parked. Her parents were probably at church already. She planned on sleeping and going to church for the evening service. Right now her bed was calling.

The owner of the vehicle got out but his truck was so high all Melanie saw was a pair of lean legs wearing light blue jeans and boots. Boots with silver tips.

She grabbed her purse, opened her car door, and exited. Maybe someone needed directions. She stuck her hand inside her purse and clutched a pen, just in case.

"Hello? Can I help you?" Melanie's tone was sharp as she rounded the vehicle with caution.

"Hello, Melanie."

Her eyes widened. Uncle stood before her. No. Not Uncle. Ted Lawson.

He stepped forward but the glare of the sun made his face hard to see. She could see he held up both hands. "Don't be alarmed. Please. I just needed to talk to you."

Sweat lined her armpits and Melanie took short

breaths. *God, You testing me already.* "Ted, why are you here?"

"I wanted to talk to you. That's all," Ted said.

Her heart hammered in her chest. She clutched her purse close to her and looked down at her sneakers. The one time she did not wear heels …

Melanie willed her feet to stand still. The urge to run inside her house was strong. Her shaky hands would not obey the simple command of putting the key inside the door.

God has slain your monster. Gary's words came back to her. Melanie relaxed before a troubling thought occurred.

"It's Chase, isn't it?" she asked. "Something happened. That's why you're here. Is he all right? Tell me what happened?" Melanie fired questions at Ted. Concern for Chase's health superseded her own fears.

Ted shook his head. "Chase is fine. I left him a couple hours ago. We spent all night in prayer."

"You did? So did I? I was praying all night with my sister. What a coincidence," Melanie said.

"That's no coincidence. That is God at work."

Melanie tilted her head. Ted was right. She stepped into the shade and gestured for Ted to step closer so she could see his face.

He looked tired and worn. This man standing before her was no monster. With a gush of air, Melanie released her fears to the wind. She squared her shoulders and turning her back to Ted, unlocked her door.

Melanie took a brave step inside and faced him. She opened her mouth, and was attacked with doubt. *No. Don't let him in. He'll hurt you.* Melanie rebuked the thoughts. *Lord, I'm trusting in You. I'm delivered. Ted's delivered. We are free.*

"Come in," she said.

With a nod, Ted entered Melanie's living space and she closed the door. She beckoned for Ted to take a seat. Seeing him curl his frame to sit on her sofa, Melanie offered a silent praise. God was still in the miracle business.

"Thank you for allowing me into your home." Ted's eyes were suspiciously wet.

Melanie's heart melted. She slid into a seat across from him and whispered, "As you said, God is at work."

Ted wrung his heads. "I'm sorry. I'm sorry. If I could undo what I did to you, I would. I was a worthless human being before God got to me. I wish I had the right words to say to you that would make you understand just how sorry I am."

Melanie nodded but tears streamed down her face blocking her view. She wiped her face with her hands so she could read Ted's lips.

"I'm here because Chase loves you and I love him. He's suffered these past months without you and to know that I ..." Ted gulped, visibly holding back tears. He touched his chest. "To know I'm contributing to Chase's pain is too much to bear. I've thought about it and if my leaving will mend your relationship, I will. If you want me to confess and do the time, I will. I've got to make this right. You and Chase belong together. I'm sure of that and I can't be the one standing in your way."

Melanie's shoulders shook. After all the crying she had done the night before, Melanie did not understand how she could produce more tears. Her body trembled but Melanie held out a hand.

Ted eye's widened.

"Take my hand," Melanie said. Her hand quivered but she was not going to back down.

With a nod, Ted reached out and placed his hands in hers.

"I forgive you," she whispered.

Ted squeezed her hand. His body vibrated. Though she could not hear it, Melanie knew Ted wailed. She waited for him to pour out before she said, "I love Chase. I want to be in his life, if he'll still have me. You and I will take baby steps."

"Thank you." Ted rose to his feet.

Melanie opened the door and came face-to-face with Chase.

"Melanie!" Chase searched her face for any signs of distress. "I didn't know he was coming. Are you all right?"

"Everything's fine, son," Ted said, stepping around Melanie and coming outside to tap him on the shoulder. "I had to talk to Melanie myself. There were things that needed to be said."

"Why didn't you say something?" While he asked his father the question, Chase kept his eyes pinned on Melanie.

"I knew you'd try to stop me," Ted said.

Melanie's smiling face put Chase at ease. It had been too long since he had seen her. He scanned her from head to toe. His wood impressions had not done her justice. She was airy, breathy, like a butterfly.

"I missed you," he said.

"I missed you, too," Melanie replied.

"I'll leave you two to talk," Ted offered, before going to his vehicle.

"Can I come in?" Chase asked.

Melanie nodded and stepped back. As soon as she closed the door, Chase pulled her into his arms. He kissed her with all the passion he had. When her arms snaked around his waist, Chase wished he could stay in that position forever. But he needed to take a breath. He was weak in the knees. Chase ended the kiss but held onto her.

Melanie licked her lips. He zoned in those pretty pink lips and groaned. He had to taste her again. Chase crushed his lips to hers and closed his eyes.

Melanie broke the kiss and pulled out of his arms.

"I love you, Chase." Her eyes served as a mirror to her heart.

He cupped her cheeks with his hands. "I love you, too," he said. "These past months have been torture.

I'm not letting you go ever again."

She smiled. "Good, because I don't intend to go anywhere."

The gift box on his passenger seat flashed into his mind. "I'll be right back," Chase said.

"Leaving already?" she teased.

Chase signed. "I have something I made for you."

She touched her heart. "You kept up with the sign language."

He nodded and signed. "You were worth every hour I spent learning to communicate with you."

"That's the best present ever. It means so much to me." She hugged him close.

It was not as good as the gift he had in the car. Chase stepped back. "I'll be back," he said, again. He rushed out of the door and retrieved the baby blue wrapped package. He held it with care and reentered Melanie's house.

Her eyes lit up and she held out her hands. Chase led her to the couch and gestured for Melanie to sit. Then he placed the box on her lap "Open it gently," he signed.

Melanie nodded. He admired her dainty fingers as she undid the white bow. Then she carefully lifted the crease of the wrapping before tearing it open. Chase felt sweat lining his forehead and upper lip and wiped his face.

Melanie removed the cover and exhaled.

His heart pounded. *Please make her like it.*

"Chase, these are beautiful," Melanie breathed out.

Chase had placed the figures in special grooves so they stood inside the box. Melanie lifted the first piece. She brought it close to her face, examining every single detail. "Wait a minute." She met his eyes. "Is this me?"

Chase nodded.

"They are exquisite," Melanie breathed. She scrutinized four of the other intricate pieces he had made. As she moved down the line of dolls, Chase felt his stomach clench with nerves. Finally, Melanie lifted the last doll. Melanie had been frozen in a swan-like prose. He had purchased a piece of white lace to serve as a scarf and resting place for the ring. He dropped to one knee and waited.

As long as he lived, Chase would never forget Melanie's wide eyes and hanging jaw when she spotted the square cut princess diamond ring. "This looks real! No! It couldn't be." She squinted her eyes. "This is a real ring."

Chase nodded. He undid the knot and held it in his right hand. Then he took her left hand. "Melanie, I knew from the moment I first saw you, you were the one for me. A lifetime is not enough for me to spend with you. Will you marry me?"

"Yes! I'd be honored to be your wife." Her eyes sparkled.

Chase slid the ring on Melanie's shaky finger. With joy in his heart, Chase rested the box with the figurines on the floor next to them. Then, he placed a possessive kiss on his fiancé's mouth. To Chase, she tasted even sweeter now that she would soon bear his name.

When their kiss ended, Melanie said, "Chase you've made me the happiest woman on the planet." She clapped her hands. "I'm so happy, I could—"

"Dance?"

Melanie nodded. Chase expected her to grab her duffel bag but Melanie surprised him. She turned on her stereo. Chase had no idea what was playing. Instead he focused on the woman beaming before him with her arms wide open.

"Dance with me," she said.

Chase stepped into Melanie's arms, and the two began their first of many dances to come.

Epilogue

"Thank you so much for coming to the first dance recital here at Rhythm & Magic Dance Studio," Melanie said into the microphone. Dressed in a special-designed studded blue leotard and matching skirt, Melanie rubbed her protruding stomach. The twins were bouncing around in there. She scanned the crowd of forty-something people. Tricia sat with Emory and bounced Amber on her lap. Melanie smiled at Amber's ballerina outfit.

Judd and Nadine waved at her and Steven signed hello. Melanie waved back at them. They had left their son, Chance, at home with a babysitter.

Next she nodded at Ted. They would never be close but they were united by their love for God. Chase had confided that Ted had finally begun dating again. She was happy for him but she was happier for herself.

Finally she blew a kiss in her parents' direction. Rhoda and Gary beamed from the sidelines. She knew how proud they were of her accomplishments.

Melanie watched the crowd begin to clap their hands as the 18 dancers entered the studio and struck a pose. Her chest puffed. Her girls would do her proud, just like she had taught them.

Janet raced inside, grabbing an empty chair in the back of the room. Melanie blew her mother a kiss.

"These young ladies have worked extremely hard to dazzle you tonight as we take you into our Winter Wonderland performance. Now sit back and enjoy the show." Melanie stepped past the fake snow and icicles. Chase had worked for two days to transform the studio to make it look like winter in the sunshine state. There were lights and white and blue balloons.

But, Melanie's favorite piece in the room was the Music, Rhythm & Magic sign. Chase had whittled each piece of the oak into letters then varnished the wood before gluing it to a wooden frame. Her treasured dancer pieces were on display in the cherry wood china case—also crafted by Chase—in her office. Every time she looked at them, she was reminded of Chase's love and devotion.

Melanie exited the stage to where Chase stood waiting and pulled him into the small cubicle. "I've got to go to the bathroom." She wiggled. "Help me before I ruin this dress you made for me," she signed.

Chase helped her with the zipper and Melanie handled her business. She sighed with relief and rose to wash her hands.

Chase laughed and drew her in for a quick kiss. Then he signed, "You have two months to go. Hang in there. Just think you'll have two more students to add to your roster soon."

Melanie laughed. It was a tight space but she felt a familiar urge.

Chase must have read her thoughts because he

shook his head. "No. Not here. We don't have enough room."

Melanie would not be swayed. She opened her arms and Chase complied. "What am I going to do with you?" he asked.

Melanie smiled. "Dance with me."

The End

Discussion Questions

1. Chase fell in love with Melanie almost from the first moment he saw her. Do you believe in love at first sight?

2. Do you think Chase was too pushy with his emotions?

3. Did you agree with Melanie and Tricia supporting Rachel?

4. Do you agree with Melanie's decision when it came to Ted?

5. Were you satisfied with the events leading up to the ending?

6. Alcoholism and addiction has far-reaching effects. Discuss these issues shaped the characters lives.

7. Dancing for Melanie was a stress reliever. What are some other healthy stress relievers?

8. Share your thoughts on Chase and Melanie's romance. Did you feel their connection?

9. What was your favorite scene?

10. Who was a standout character?

About the Author

Michelle Lindo-Rice is the bestselling author of "Able to Love" and "On the Right Path" series. She enjoys crafting women's fiction with themes centered around the four "F" words: Faith, Friendship, Family and Forgiveness. She was nominated for Author of the Year 2014 in Building Relationships Around Books book club. Michelle's first published work, Sing A New Song, was a Black Expressions Editor's Choice featured selection. My Steps Are Ordered, the second book in the "On the Right Path" series made the AALBC bestseller lists on May/June 2014 and August/September 2014. My Steps Are Ordered was also #1 in UBAWA's 2014 Top 100 list. The Fall of the Prodigal made #2 on Black Christian Reads Fiction List for March 2015.

Her published books are:

Sing a New Song (Feb. 2013) This was featured as an Editor's Choice in Black Expressions Book Club.

Walk a Straight Line (Jan. 2014)

Color Blind (May 2014)

My Steps are Ordered (Aug. 2014)

Unbound Hearts (Dec. 2014)

The Fall of the Prodigal (Jan. 2015)

Silent Praise (Spring 2015)

My Soul Then Sings (Sept. 2015)

Please connect with her at:

Website: www.michellelindorice.com (Please join her mailing list)

Catch up with Michelle at Linkedin, Facebook, YouTube, Twitter, Pinterest, StumbledUpon, Google+, BlackChristianReads.com, AALBC, Wattpad, Tumblr

41410278R00155

Made in the USA
Charleston, SC
30 April 2015